R K E

K   S E A   U.S.S.R

Samsun

Trabzon   Kars

→ •Amasya   ^^^^^^ ^ ^ ^ ^ ^
E. Karadeniz Mts.   ^^^^^^^
Çoruh
Mts.

•Reşadiya   R. Euphrates   Erzurum   Mt.Arat
^

R. Kızılırmak   L.Keban ^^^^^^^   ^
L.Va

←•Kayseri   ^
eme   R.Tigris   Hakkari Mts.
^Mt.Erciyes   ^^^^^^^^
^ ^

^
^Aladağ
Adana
Marsin   I R A G

•Antakya   S Y R I A

⟶   Ben's Voyage
⟶   Boris's Journey

Memoirs of a Turkish Bear

and of the English boy who loved him

Rozelle Raynes

For my racing-car man

Who took me on such a memorable journey around the coast and
across the wondrous mountains of Southern Turkey.....

Memoirs of a Turkish Bear

and of the English boy who loved him

Rozelle Raynes

With drawings by the author and a painting by Abigail Webster

Castweasel Publishing

Castweasel Publishing.
Thoresby Park
Newark, Notts.
NG22 9EP

ISBN 9780954746728

Published by Castweasel Publishing.
Enquiries etc. to Thoresby Exhibition Centre
Thoresby Park, Newark, Notts NG22 9EP.

Designed by Off The Wall Associates
www.offthewallassociates.com

Printed by Oyster Press
sales@oysterpress.co.uk

Foreword

The subject of dancing bears in Turkey is liable to arouse strong feelings of anger for many people. The cruelty to animals and the sheer horror of forcing such lovable beasts to perform on their hind legs for the amusement of us selfish mortals! It hardly bears thinking about.

But not all dancing bears are ill-treated or forced to lead unhappy lives. A few, in fact, earn money for their families and applause for themselves. Those ones are usually regarded like much-loved dogs might be in England, and I have seen some driving around Istanbul in a *Dolmuş* (6-seater taxi) with their cheerful owners on the seat beside them.

Everything depends on their master's character. Some will strap a painful harness around their heads and across their faces, give them very little food and beat them with a cane if they refuse to rise onto their back legs and dance to the rhythm of the tambourine: whereas others will treat their bears like old friends without whom they could not survive with any degree of happiness.

Our Boris was a brave intelligent bear who grew up with a loving family of Nomads in the Taurus Mountains...

CONTENTS

Acknowledgments

My special thanks to John Gammons whose hard work and inspiration helped me to produce this unusual story...

And to Abigail Webster whose lovely painting of Boris catching a fish is a very special addition to the narrative.

Prologue

He sat on top of the sunkissed hill and guzzled a slice of water-melon. The juice ran down his cheeks in two meandering streams until it finally came to rest in the collar of his clean blue shirt. He paused from time to time, his tongue arranged like a catapult, and a purple melon-seed shot forth to land with deadly accuracy on a mound of earth in front of him; then he leant forward eagerly to watch the diligent red ants carry it away to their secret kingdom beyond the ridge.

Ben Merrick was sixteen. Tall and sturdily built, he had wiry brown hair, gentle grey eyes concealed behind severe National Health spectacles and a firm square chin that enhanced his good-natured expression. It was all so utterly different here from home and Ben felt a tingling sensation in his veins - as if something quite extraordinary was about to happen. He gazed in wonder at the slender minarets floating in the heat haze above the shining waters of the Golden Horn, and listened to the freighters and ferry-boats blaring away with their deep-throated sirens to vie with the motor-horns of a thousand ancient taxi-cabs all over the sprawling city.

He examined the world around him with the questing eyes of a child of seven or eight, a well-mannered obedient child who seldom gave trouble to his parents. His father, who considered himself a classical scholar of distinction, had set off early that morning on a tour of Byzantine relics in the old city of Stamboul across the Golden Horn. His mother, meanwhile, had brought him to the park and given him the strictest instructions to wait on the hill for her return, while she slipped away to the shops near the Hilton Hotel to buy herself a glamorous new dress. Partly to lull her own conscience, she had left him a tasty snack to eat when he felt hungry: two rolls oozing butter and honey, filched from the hotel breakfast table; two large slices of water-melon and a bottle of peach juice, everything packed neatly in a plastic bag.

Ben was very happy on his hill. A stiff breeze blew down the Bosphorus and the branches of a eucalyptus tree came to life, their shadows leaping to and fro across his outstretched legs. Somewhere far below him, at some invisible watery crossroads concealed behind the tall buildings along the waterfront, the Golden Horn, the Sea of Marmara and the Bosphorus flowed into one another, creating a vast merry-go-round of swirling currents; and the liners with their tugs, the pilot-boats and the ferries sped across the dancing waves, each one intensely alive and singing a special song to celebrate that glorious spring morning.

Ben grinned broadly because he felt warm and excited. Suddenly, however, his expression changed as his attention became riveted upon two figures in the small wood below him. A man wearing a grubby cloth cap, a sheepskin waistcoat over a grey woollen shirt and a pair of baggy black trousers that hung in a loose pouch at the back, was sitting down under a pine tree; and as soon as he had settled comfortably he closed his eyes. A large dog with shabby brown fur slumped down beside him, its face hidden from sight between its two front paws. The boy supposed that they had walked a long way under the warm April sun and felt very hot and tired.

Ben had always longed to possess a dog of his own - a big furry animal which would follow him wherever he went and gaze at him with liquid brown eyes filled with devotion. He had never cared for cats - too independent and remote by far - but a dog was another matter altogether. Ma had no strong feelings one way nor the other, and would probably have given in had not Pa taken a firm stance right from the beginning. "Dogs are dirty germ-spreading beasts!" he declared severely. "No child of mine is going to run the risk of playing with such verminous creatures."

So that was that. But it was no passing whim for Ben, and the longing for a dog with which to share his life grew in his child's brain at the same rate as his body grew to manhood; until a tiny seed of resentment against his father took root and flourished discordantly among all the respectable seeds so carefully nurtured by his mother.

The man resting under the tree must have felt Ben's eyes boring into his companion, for he stirred uneasily and looked up at the boy on the summit of the hill. He then prodded his beast with the toe of his right foot and whispered urgently; "Wake up, little brother! This is no time to slumber. One of the infidel tourists sits yonder on the top of the hill and he regards thee with the eyes of a lover! He has money and to spare, of that one may be certain. Let us arise and see how much we can extract from his foolish purse."

There was a considerable commotion as the Turk's companion rose to his paws, grunting noisily and tugging peevishly at his lead; then continued to rise higher and higher until he stood on his hind paws six feet tall, with his mouth wide open and the bell attached to his collar clanging vigorously.

Thus they slowly advanced towards the boy on the hill, and the man beat a strange rhythm on a tambourine while the beast danced a lumbering type of polka, simultaneously clapping his front paws together in time with the music. The Turk's expression, Ben decided, was distinctly fierce; those unblinking reddish-brown eyes the colour of melon-seeds, the glowering black eyebrows and moustache to match, the latter framing a rat-trap of a mouth. Ben was spellbound. Trembling with fear and excitement he realized that this was no dog, but a large brown bear polkaring towards him. He stood up and became aware of the sweat flowing freely from every pore in his skin causing numerous tickles in awkward places; so he lifted up his left arm and began to scratch an offending arm-pit with his right fingernails - a nasty habit Ma thought she had quite eliminated.

The bear was used to tourists buzzing round with their silly cameras, but not to a big primitive child like this one. He suddenly stopped dancing and began to investigate his own left arm-pit with the claws of his right front paw. Ben threw back his head and roared with laughter - a deep-throated belly laugh that pleased the bear - and the animal continued to scratch itself more emphatically, baring a mouthful of gigantic yellowish teeth. Ben knelt down and extracted the two buns filled with butter and honey and the last slice of water-melon from his plastic bag and, walking fearlessly down the hill, he offered them to the bear and his master. The Turk was very touched by this gesture.

"He behaves more like a follower of the True Prophet, sharing his sustenance with strangers," he told the bear. And he looked deeply into the boy's eyes and understood much of his life story.

At that moment there was a deafening screech from above. Ma had returned and taken in at one glance the domestic scene at the foot of the hill; but she had lost all control of her vocal chords as a wave of guilt and fear swept over her and threatened to choke her. Ben swung round and saw her and, although he was just beginning to enjoy himself, his sense of filial devotion and obedience was so strong that he dared not linger; so he began to amble rather dejectedly back up the hill. A fleeting thought passed through his mother's mind as she watched him: "God, they're like brothers, those two! A bear on a lead with his keeper, and a human bear on an invisible lead with his keeper. Each one trained to dance to a certain tune..."

She never liked to have such thoughts but sometimes they crowded into her troubled mind, unwanted and unheralded. As soon as he came within reach she grabbed hold of Ben's arm and hurried him away to the safety of the crowded streets, the blaring car-horns and the welcoming swing doors of their hotel.

He looked back over one shoulder as they came to the edge of the park and saw the bear sitting peacefully under a tree eating his bun while his master devoured the slice of water-melon. Ben had the impression, although it was too far away to be quite sure, that the Turk's eyes looked much softer than before - they no longer reminded him of melon-seeds but seemed more like velvety purple grapes; rather friendly grapes, if it were possible to imagine such a thing. And the bear, who was watching him closely, licked one of his paws appreciatively then waved - yes, actually waved goodbye to the astonished boy.

Chapter I

Those Who Walk

(Boris's Story)

The Master is squatting under a eucalyptus tree smoking his *narghile*. It makes hubble-bubble noises as he puffs into it, and brings a far-away look to his eyes. Wisps of smoke go spiralling up and up into the evening sky; and he is beginning to smile round the corners of his mouth - perhaps he thinks of that boy with the big laugh who shared his victuals so readily with strangers?

"Well, I liked him too so I shall not grumble if we meet him again."

We have been here for an hour or more and my belly is empty and rumbling noisily, so I bump the Master's elbow as if by accident, to remind him of my existence...

"I heard thee, little brother;" his face splits into a wide grin. "There is no need to prod me thus! Arise, Boris thou clumsy bear, and we will return to our lodgings so that I can prepare thy forage. "He scratches my head, just behind the left ear where it tickles best; and I amble along beside him down the steep hill towards old Stamboul and the setting sun.

As we move through the narrow streets the Master talks to me; although I cannot answer him in human language, he knows that I understand.

"I have a yearning in my bones to return to the tribe from whence we came," he murmurs softly. "Too long have we stayed in this dusty city surrounded by people scurrying to and fro like half-crazed ants. Thy fur is dry and shabby, my poor Boris, and it is time that we inhaled again the pure mountain air and found a place where thou canst eat thy fill of young azalea roots, hazel-nuts and honey, instead of this meagre city fare."

I watch his face closely and notice a gleam of excitement in his eyes and a firm set to his chin as he strides across Galata Bridge to the other side of the Golden Horn. Then we turn right, and after a while begin to climb upwards towards the Mosque of Sultan Selim. The district where we lodge is a poor run-down area - no tourists, nor big hotels and fine shops; but the people are kind and friendly and we were lucky to have found such a cosy den, especially during the long cold months of winter.

I can see Mr Yussef's stall at the next crossroads, surrounded by a cluster of workmen buying fruit and vegetables for their evening meals. The *Bey* and his assistant are peeling small cucumbers and splitting them down the middle as we approach, and the Master prods me sharply in the ribs and gives me a significant look.

"Aha! What a fine bear you have *Arif Bey* Effendi," smiles the boss, while his boy gurgles like a mountain stream.

I have risen on to my hind paws and am dancing a cha-cha in front of the Master, while I wave my front paws in the air and pretend that I am a Spanish female clicking castanets!

"Allow me to present you and your gifted companion with a few cucumbers," says Mr Yussef. "It is a rare pleasure to see such talent in this quarter." The Master accepts with a dignified bow and his most engaging smile. We carefully ignore each other till we have rounded the next corner; then I leap into the air several times and the Master runs his fingers through my fur and whispers lovingly; "What a clever bear thou art! We shall never starve while thou canst dance."

Presently we come to our house, a ramshackle wooden dwelling leaning in a sociable manner towards its neighbour; in fact, our roof actually touches the other one, as if it wished to communicate some dark secrets. Most of it is painted turquoise-blue, and it has a small verandah on the top floor where the landlord smokes his pipe on hot summer nights.

My den is in a shed at the back, a cool dark place with fresh straw stacked in a corner. The Master now spreads some of it around the stone floor after he has raked over the dirty stuff and shovelled it into a plastic bag. He fills my big drinking-bowl with water, cuts up half the cucumbers that Mr Yussef gave us and mixes them with stale bread, a few old potatoes and roots and a chunk of goat's cheese; then he opens the door to his private cupboard - in which I am never allowed to delve - and extracts a small slice of *baklava* (like shredded wheat soaked in honey) and stands there holding it in a tantalizing way while I gobble up the contents of my bowl; it only takes me a few seconds and I am still hungry when I have finished.

"This is a special treat for being such an intelligent bear," he says, handing me the tiny sweet morsel - how I wish it were the size of a pumpkin!

*　　*　　*　　*

The *muezzin* has already called the faithful to evening prayer, so the Master has gone to the Mosque of Sultan Selim and I am curled up in the fresh straw feeling drowsy and contented; but not so drowsy that I failed to pick up the vibrations of momentous happenings in the air. These have set me thinking about my life and first beginnings, and the day when the Master found me as a tiny cub...

It was on a cold autumn morning high up in the Taurus Mountains when my mother left our cave in search of food. I was only a few days old, a fat cub with half-opened eyes gazing anxiously at the strange world outside our home, and I was desperately afraid whenever she left me alone. That huge reassuring presence with her warm brown pelt and mouth full of big white teeth that laughed at my silly baby ways; but I knew that she would guard me with her life if need be.

Well, that's just what happened when the party of hunters strolled past our cave and she leapt in front of the entrance so that no one should see me inside. The hunters smirked with glee as they shot my mother with a dozen bullets and carried her bleeding body away on their shoulders. I saw a man on the far side of the track watch them with narrowed eyes of hatred set in a stern unsmiling face; then I began to cry and cry until I thought my heart would break.

Suddenly a big dog came snuffling into the cave and nudged me gently, breaking through my barrier of misery; then he went away and I felt worse than ever, more completely abandoned, until the man with the stern face was brought to the cave by that same dog - Albay, they called him. He trotted in and began to lick my face to stop me crying, and the man bent down and picked me up in his arms and carried me away from the place where I was born.

"Look, Zenda, what Albay has found for us!" he exclaimed to a young woman who was waiting by a Tartar wagon with big wheels, its sides decorated with red and yellow roses.

"Oh, the poor lonely baby!" she cried. "I'll give him some warm milk and honey, and put him in the cart to sleep with our own babies." And that was how the two best years of my life began...

After a few weeks my new family told their friends that I was a gentle trusting animal, but rather showy, as I loved to make the tribesmen laugh by jumping around on my hind legs and waving my front paws in the air; so they decided to call me Boris after a famous politician.

Arif, my Master, was a Turcoman nomad, known as a *Yörük* (it means "Those Who Walk") by the people settled on the plains. His ancestors had walked all the way to Anatolia from the frozen steppes of Siberia some three hundred years ago, and even to this day he and his family continued to live in a black goat-hair tent surrounded by their flocks of sheep and goats. Every spring they would trek up to the *'yaylas'*, or summer pastures, high up on the mountain slopes where there was plenty of water for flocks; and in the cool days of autumn, just at the season when the Master found me in the cave, they returned to their winter quarters in some sheltered valley near the warm coastal plain. Naturally I knew none of these facts as a young cub, but Albay, the Karabaş dog, told me much of interest about our family as I grew to be a teen-age bear.

"The Master was different to all the other men in our tribe," he explained to me one day. "The others prided themselves on their skill as fearless hunters, especially the Master's father, Abdul Kiazim. But Arif was a dreamy unpractical boy who took after his mother, and loved nothing better than to lie on his back in the grass and gaze at the glittering snow-clad summits and the eagles circling high above the rocky pinnacles.

'That boy is altogether too soft,' Abdul Kiazim would complain to his wife from time to time. 'And he is completely besotted with animals and treats them as his personal friends! We must strive to make a man of him and teach him the harsh laws of reality.'

Abdul's wife bowed her head meekly, for she would not have dared to contradict her husband; but, secretly, she hoped that her son would never change for already he had developed a rare affinity with all weak and defenceless creatures, whether animal or human, and was, surprisingly, a great favourite among the nomads in the rough camps where they lived.

"How, then," I asked the dog; "did he manage to survive with such a father, and in such tough surroundings?"

"Well, you see," murmured Albay, fluffing out his fur and causing his tail to arch over his back till it resembled the full moon; "that was partly due to my influence! The Master grew to manhood on the harsh mountainsides surrounded by men of granite, but his character did not change; and no one ever saw him kill a beast with his own hands. The tribesmen could not deny, however, that he had grown into the finest goatherd in living memory. He and I would vanish for weeks on end with the flock, but he always refused the weapons his father pressed upon him, saying that his goatherd's crook was all he needed."

I gazed at my companion with grave respect. I realized that much of what he told me was way above my head, a simple bear cub with no worldly experience, but I loved to listen to his gruff voice and the words of wisdom that escaped from his mouth.

Albay (the name means Colonel) was an enormous powerful dog with a short cream-coloured coat and a black muzzle and ears His golden-brown eyes, set wide apart in his broad skull, radiated loyalty and intelligence, and he often wore a spiked collar to protect his throat from the onslaught of wolves.

"The Master and I would disappear with our flock," Albay continued; "finding secret pastures in remote parts of the mountains where the goats and sheep could graze peacefully and grow fat, while we ourselves lived on goat's milk, azalea blossom, hazel-nuts and all sorts of strange herbs that grew in the most unlikely places. Those were the best days of our lives, living together under the searing summer sun and the brilliant stars at night on the slopes of a great mountain called the Ala Dagh. We never lost a single sheep or goat during those lonely vigils, although we were sometimes attacked by wild beasts from the forest... wolves, jackals and even bears."

I noticed a proud gleam in the dog's eyes when he reached this part of his story, and an extra arch to his tail.

"Because of this," Albay continued; "the Master's parents came to believe that their son lived under the special protection of Allah. And at last Abdul Kiazim's heart grew wise with age so that he no longer urged Arif to become a hunter like himself."

On another day Albay told me about how his Master had first met Zenda, the beautiful Tartar girl from the lowlands. She was selling water-melons on the outskirts of a humble village near the sea-shore, but her eyes were restless and sad because she yearned for the high mountains and her family had settled permanently on that dull humid plain.

Arif's heart was filled with love as he gazed at her from the back of his tall camel, and to the simple village girl he appeared like a prince dropped down from the sky.

I noticed a certain reticence, perhaps a hint of jealousy, as the dog mentioned casually that the Master married her that winter and brought her back to the mountains in the springtime, riding behind him on his camel. Then children began to arrive: first she gave birth to a male child - Hasan, they called him; and a year or two later, his baby sister, Djenan, was born in a cave (like me!) in the foothills of the Taurus Mountains.

Albay's voice had, by this time, become quite sullen and grumpy, and I could sense how he had suffered with that woman and those two human babies taking up the Master's time and

claiming his affection, so that he had hardly any left for his devoted old companion. But for me it was quite a different story: I had been reared myself by the tender and loving hands of Zenda, beside her own babies who were like a brother and sister to me. After the Master, they were the human beings I loved the most. Never a day passed without Zenda finding some wild honey to spread on my Juniper roots, and the children were always looking for presents to give me so that I would feel happy and a part of their family.

Why, I remember so clearly the day Hasan was dressed up in his very best clothes, to go to Adana with his mother and grandfather, to sell the fine black wool, from our Angora goats. He wore a red wool shirt with a green, mauve and pink pullover, knitted by his mother for special occasions; in his new intensely smart white linen trousers - but the trouble was they would keep slipping down when he least expected it! Finally Zenda had insisted on his wearing his warm mauve cardigan in case the evening grew cold. Just before they were due to leave he briefly disappeared into the woods for a minute, and returned holding a pretty bunch of flowers.

"These are for you, Boris," he said, giving me such a searching look, as if he wanted to remember my startled furry face for ever and ever.

I felt restless and desperately anxious after the party had left, carrying the wool in saddle-bags slung across the backs of our two camels. The Master shared my mood and neither of us could settle down to sleep that night.

Next morning a *jandarma* came to our camp to tell us there had been an accident on the road to Adana: a lorry had swerved while rounding a sharp bend and had run over and killed Zenda and her son, who were walking behind Abdul Kiazim's camel. The Master's heart turned to ice, and for many months he lived inside a lonely grey cloud which was never pierced by the warm rays of the sun.

He longed to leave his tribe and the great mountains that he and Zenda had loved so dearly, so that he could nurse his broken heart among strangers. Arif's ageing parents understood his sorrow and agreed to care for Albay and the little girl, Djenan, during his

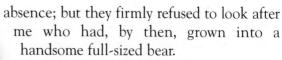

absence; but they firmly refused to look after me who had, by then, grown into a handsome full-sized bear.

"Why not allow me to shoot him, and the money thou couldst get for his pelt would stand thee in good stead on thy travels?" suggested Abdul Kiazim.

But the bleak look had returned to the Master's eyes and his mouth was as hard and uncompromising as a molewrench. He strode out of the camp pulling me along behind him on a leather lead, but when we came to the village down in the valley I hung back for a moment, as I had noticed our Djenan sitting under a ring-bolt outside the shepherd's house. I wanted to go to her and comfort her for she looked so small and lonely; but the Master gave a sharp tug at my lead, appearing not to notice her, and soon we were through the village and hurrying across the open countryside.

After many hard and hungry weeks on the road during the sweltering summer months, the Master and I came at last to the great city of Istanbul where, he had been assured, a man with such a fine bear could make his fortune among the foreign tourists. But my Master had no head for business; he often, in fact, encouraged me to dance for nothing if our audience happened to be children or poor people from the suburbs. And when we did manage to earn some money he was often foolishly extravagant: one evening I developed a sore paw and, just imagine, he insisted on waiting at a taxi rank for a private cab to take us home!

When, at last, we reached the Mecca of dancing bears, the Topkapi Palace gardens and the surroundings of St Sophia and the Blue Mosque, we found all the pitches already occupied by men from Thrace with small inferior bears, men who glared at us with angry eyes and refused to let us share their rich pickings from the hordes of tourists who came there, day after day.

But all those matters are in the past; a hundred thousand years ago it sometimes seems to me. We have managed to survive by hovering around such places as the football stadium, the weekly market in Çarsamba and the cheaper types of restaurants along the shores of the Bosphorus. Not the grandest of pitches one has to admit, but we made many friends among the people in our audiences; and I have a feeling that this phase of our life is over.

My eyes are closing fast, I can hear the Master's footsteps in our alleyway, and tomorrow... who knows where we shall go?

Chapter II

Embarkation Day

(Ben's Story)

Today is a very special day - Embarkation Day, Pa calls it - and I am going for a voyage on a big ship for the first time in my life. I don't know much about the sea and ships but I felt so excited that I could hardly sleep last night, and I woke up before sunrise when the man with the strange voice sang out from the house with a helmet-shaped roof across the road. Then an extraordinary thing happened: a host of men from far away took up his song, and it spread like angel's music for miles and miles across the sleeping city.

I like being here for everything is so different from at home. No one stares at me then turns away to snigger behind my back; nor tells me what to do with an extra loud clear voice, as if I mightn't understand them otherwise. Either they ignore me here, or they give me nice friendly looks - like the bear man did in the end.

We have been here for two or three weeks now and Pa goes off to visit museums and old ruins most days, but he won't take us with him as he says it's all rather above our heads. Ma doesn't mind as she prefers to go shopping and I have to trail around with her. She never leaves me on my own any more in case I should go back to that park where I met the bear. I want to go there again more than anywhere else, but Pa was very angry when he heard about my adventure and has strictly forbidden her to take me there, or to mention the subject again.

A funny thing happened last night, all the same. Pa said he would take us to a nice little restaurant on the Bosphorus for dinner as a special treat. We caught a steamer to this place - an old boat with lots of black smoke belching out of its funnel. I watched it leave the pier after we had landed and it looked like a dream-boat in the twilight, the reflections of its lights zigzagging across the dark water and people's heads outlined against the brightness of the windows as it pulled away from the shore. Then the steamer gave a great blast on its whistle and I jumped in the air with surprise; if Ma had not grabbed me by the seat of my pants, I'm sure I should have fallen into the water.

The restaurant was lovely. Red table-cloths, red benches and red lanterns above us that glowed like rubies in the night. I loved being there and the food was delicious. Ma and Pa were enjoying themselves too when a nice man sitting on a seat nearby came across to talk to us.

"I hope a good visit to this city you are having?" he asked us. "And my country happiness to you brings."

Pa smiled (he is used to this back- to-front way they speak here) and began to tell him about all the marvellous things he'd seen in Istanbul.

The man seemed very pleased, and he chatted with Pa for a few minutes before turning to me and saying; "Last week at this restaurant you should have been, young man, for a sight to cause pleasure it was possible to see - perhaps in England a sight you have never seen?"

Then he told us about a man with a big brown bear who danced in front of the people while they ate their dinners. My ears twitched like a rabbit's ears to catch every word he uttered, but Pa suddenly turned funny and sprang to his feet calling for the bill, although Ma still had some wine in her glass. As soon as he had paid he hurried us away, hardly bothering to say goodbye to our new friend; and we had to jump on to another steamer that was just leaving to go back to Istanbul.

A few minutes later Pa began to feel a bit guilty about his bad behaviour, I think, so he said; "As soon as we land I'll take you to a place where you can see a touch of magic, if you like?"

Ma squeezed my arm as she knew he was only doing it to

make up for rushing us away from the restaurant. But when we reached this special place Ma and I gasped with the wonder of it all... A colossal helmet-topped building with four spiked sentinels - "It's called a mosque, Ben," Pa explained; "a place where the Turks go to say their prayers," - had turned itself into a gold and silver dream above the dark night trees; and below it were tall buildings and street-lamps that glittered like stars and, best of all, OUR ship! She's called the M. S. *Zonguldak*, and she has three rows of diamond windows and a fat red, white and yellow funnel with crossed anchors in the middle of it.

Long straight avenues of green, orange, silver and gold reflections came shimmering across the Golden Horn to meet us, and I tried putting a foot in the water to see what colour it would turn; but Pa told me not to be so silly and Ma began to scold me because one of my new shoes was squelching wet. After that, we returned to our hotel and went to bed.

The coach comes for us after breakfast and we drive quickly downhill to a place called Karakoy. I have my nose pressed up against the window-pane, searching everywhere for that park. Ma annoys me because she will keep tugging at my sleeve and asking me what I'm looking for, but I think it is safer not to answer her. Far too many people ask and ask their silly questions; if you tell them the truth, however, they cluck like hens and a peculiar look comes into their eyes, then they go in search of another grown-up person to whisper secrets into their ears.

Here we are, on the water's edge at last. It's all heaving and shining, brown silver and grey, with steamers hooting to tell you they're about to leave and big ships churning up the water, and the outlines of mosques and minarets standing out darkly against the brightness in the sky.

Ma perches herself on top of a baggage-truck to get a good look at the other passengers waiting for the ship, so I walk over to the water's edge and sit down beside Pa on a big iron mushroom. Suddenly our ship comes into view, making a deep grunting noise on her whistle - Pa calls it a siren - and I can feel a buzz of excitement all round me.

"Now that's what I call a proper ship, Ben," Pa says happily. "A decent-shaped hull, tall masts and derricks, a sensible funnel and plenty of open decks for the passengers. Quite different from some of those modern abortions where you can't tell the bow from the stern, and all the decks are glassed in and stuffed with supermarkets and fruit machines."

I don't know much about ships, proper or otherwise, and I try hard to imagine what he means by 'abortion', a word I've never heard before. But I feel proud to be sharing this mushroom with Pa while he talks to me in this way, like one intelligent man to another. It reminds me of the great day last year when I brought home my first wages and put them into Ma's lap; sixty pounds at the end of the week for sweeping the floors and yard, emptying the bins and tidying up at the chemical factory near our home. Ma hugged me and declared that I was now a grown-up man, and she was more proud of me than she could say.

Mind you, I know it's not much of a job compared with other people's jobs; but already they've given me a small rise after one year, and I once overheard the boss tell a factory inspector that I was always so punctual and reliable, he really didn't know how he'd get along without me. That went to my head like a glass of champagne! It made me feel that I might be some use in this world after all, despite what people say when they think I'm out of earshot.

Our ship - you can see her name now - edges carefully in towards the land, and Pa and I have to leave our mushroom as some sailors have come to put a big loop of rope over the top of it. Everyone pushes forward at once to try and be the first up the steep wooden stairs ("Gangway, you silly boy," corrects Pa) on to the ship.

When we reach the top there are so many new and exciting things to watch that I just stand there and gape: I can see a yellow giraffe dangling a red car from its teeth; and some dark-skinned sailors are laughing and joking as they tie canvas covers over the square gaps in the deck; and something is rumbling and throbbing under my feet, like a giant monster breathing... whatever can it be? Dozens of little gulls squawk outside a half-open door from which comes a hungry-making smell of fried onions. And there's a beautiful NEW smell! I ask Ma and she asks the man behind her, who says it's tarred rope.

A tall man wearing a snow-white shirt comes towards us; he has black hair, eyebrows, moustache and trousers, and they stand out most strikingly against his shirt. He takes charge of us, shows us to our cabins, finds our luggage and says he hopes we will be very comfortable and enjoy our voyage. Also he tells us that his name is Mustafa, and if there is anything we want, just call for Mustafa in a loud voice!

Then he bows to Ma and bares his teeth in a dazzling smile, before gently closing the door.

Pa furrows his eyebrows and grunts, so I say the first thing that enters my head to take his mind off Mustafa.

"I do like this ship and the little round window over my bed," I say. "I'll be able to watch the sea rush by at night from there."

Pa tells me that the round window is called a porthole, and I must try to learn the proper words for things on a ship. And Ma gives me a special look - a look that tells me how clever she thinks I am, sometimes...

Five great blasts on the ship's siren, so we hurry out on deck to see what is happening. A stern-faced man with his cap and jacket trimmed with gold braid is standing high above us, stamping with impatience.

"Look! There's the Captain on his bridge," Ma whispers urgently. "He's the most important man on the ship, Ben."

Pa begins to look bristly again, so I move away to watch the two tugs fussing round the M.S. *Zonguldak* like sheep-dogs as she pulls away from the land. A few passengers are waving to shore people and dabbing at their eyes, but a thin man wearing a hard egg-shaped hat flings out his arms and bursts into song. I move nearer because I like his face and the way he sings, but a stuffy Englishwoman we met on the aeroplane from London glares at him in a nasty way.

"He must be drunk!" she hisses to the man beside her. "Fancy allowing an exhibition like that before the voyage has even started."

Turkish people are gathering around the singer, laughing and clapping, so I move closer, ignoring the woman who reminds me of a frozen fish finger. Suddenly the singer notices me and sings a few words specially for me alone. This makes me blush and feel embarrassed - but rather pleased, all the same. I decide, however, to move away to the other side of the ship in case Ma or Pa should find me here.

It is the magic hour. In the distance there is a great bridge - the one joining Europe with Asia, Pa told me this morning - and it hangs like a jewelled necklace above the swift flowing water. A coal ship is puffing black smoke into the sky as she steams towards the bridge and the houses on the Europe side beyond the ship are pink and mauve, like a jigsaw puzzle; but on the Asia side it's all on fire with the rays of the setting sun glinting from a thousand window-panes and the mosques(I've remembered what they're

called!) outlined in a grand way against the crimson sky.

Our ship swings round onto a new course, so I move to the other side of the deck to have one more look at Istanbul. It's like a dream city with all those fantastic shapes fading away into the twilight and a tall lighthouse sending its warning flashes across the dark water. There are ships of all sizes at anchor, ferry-boats hurrying to and fro, fishing-boats heading the same way as us, each with one djenan and one emerald eye winking at me; and any number of little rowing-boats, whichever way you look.

I glance back for the last time and think of the bear and his master, and wonder if I shall ever see them again. My elbows are planted on the ship's rail and I cup my face in my hands to cut out the things that are closest to me; but my glasses have become so misted over that I can no longer tell the difference between the ship's red flag with its white star and new moon and the gold loom in the sky behind it, which is all that is left of the magic city. Then Ma creeps up in bedroom slippers and begins to tug at my sleeve...

Chapter III
The Road To The Mountains
(Boris's Story)

The *muezzin* is calling the faithful to evening prayer. The Master attaches my lead to an iron ring on the bank overlooking the Bosphorus, and goes into the mosque behind us. I squat on my haunches and gaze at the fast-flowing water swirling under the bridge and the green and silver lights dotted among the trees on the far side. There is also a line of gold lamps all the way across the bridge, each one the same size and distance from its brother, like soldiers on parade. I doze a little and watch the lights dancing in the purple water...

"They say it's the longest bridge in Europe, Boris." The Master has crept up behind me and is scratching my ears. "And it's the only one in the world linking two continents."

I nod my head politely, but I am not really interested in such matters, especially at the end of such a long hard day. We were up at dawn to pack our belongings - the few things that were not too heavy to carry on the Master's back; all the other household essentials like my big drinking-bowl, the pots and pans for cooking and the Master's bed and chairs we gave to our friends around the Sultan Selim quarter, the people who have been kind to us during our stay in Istanbul.

"Now we must do a full day's work to earn some money for the road, my lazy bear," said the Master, "then we will cross the great bridge at night when the traffic has died down."

We tramped uphill to the market-place in Çarşamba where I danced till my back legs ached; then downhill to Sirkeci Railway Station where the passengers coming from the continental express trains were too tired or bad-tempered to wish to see me dance. Later we crossed Galata Bridge, heading for the shores of the Bosphorus. My armpits began to itch and suddenly I longed, just for a few minutes, to have the power of human speech; then I might have persuaded the Master to return to that park where we found the boy with the big laugh sitting on a hill eating a water-melon.

I know that he would like to meet the boy again who, in some strange way, was responsible for starting us on our travels today. But everything that happens in our lives is the will of Allah, according to my Master, and he would never dream of giving a hint here and there to help Allah arrange things in a manner to please us also.

I tugged hard on my lead, aiming towards the park, but the Master had no knowledge of what I wished him to do so he tugged the opposite way.

"Thou art straining my arms, Boris," he admonished me. "There is no point in climbing that steep hill. We will go to the restaurant by the ferry-station where we might find a few early clients."

As I said before, it has been a long hard day, and had it not been for the generosity of Mr Yussef who gave us a big bag of cucumbers and bananas as a parting gift, we should be very hungry as well as tired by now.

*   *   *   *

I am just beginning to doze off after my supper when I feel my left ear being pulled and hear the Master's voice announcing very distinctly; "It's time to cross the bridge, little brother. Wake up and rub the sleep from thine eyes!"

We scramble up a rough embankment, then a long flight of stone steps on to the bridge. I dare say it is the quietest time to cross, but there are still some murderous lorries hurtling over the bridge on their way to Ankara, and we feel like helpless insects clinging to the parapet for fear of being ground to pulp under their gigantic wheels. The Master is as frightened as I am - I can tell by the sweat on his hands as he grips my collar and whispers soothing words in my ears.

Perhaps he remembers Zenda and little Hasan, and wonders how it would feel to perish under the belly of one of those stinking monsters.

A long black ship passes beneath us near the centre of the bridge. It has two white lights on a pole planted in its chest, a green one on its right flank and a red one on its left. A group of men are standing on a raised platform looking up at the bridge and one of them points at me and laughs, so I wave to him; then I notice another small light on the ship's tail. A moment later there is nothing but creamy water, bubbling and hissing; the last ripples die away and the Bosphorus is still and silent again. I crane my neck towards Russia but there is nothing, nothing left to see. The black ship has come and gone, and now the shades of twilight are fast closing in.

At last we reach the steps on the far side of the bridge and I go leaping down them, four at a time. We pause on the corner for the Master to put some *kurus* into a blind man's bowl, then we race each other to the bottom and he dances me round and round on my hind legs and tells me he has brought a special treat for me, to celebrate our return to Asia. And, guess what? He pulls a big chunk of *baklava* out of his pocket and hands it to me with a deep bow, as if I were a prince!

We are standing in a long street called Paşa Limani Caddesi, and we dive under the bridge that roars above us, and head off into the dark night along the east shore of the Bosphorus. The Master is in a talkative mood and tells me that he has heard of an inlet filled with old boats below the castle at Anadolu Hisar, and we will make for this place as we might be able to sleep in one of them tonight.

"It's only about three kilometres away," he tells me; "and it would be a new experience for thee, Boris, to be rocked to sleep by the waves!"

It seems a long three kilometres to me, and we have to jump off the road into the bushes each time a car comes speeding round a sharp bend and blinds us with its head-lights.

It is long after midnight when we finally reach the village and search around for the inlet. I can hear the water sucking and gurgling beneath a small bridge, and presently the Master helps me into a big wooden bowl that tilts under my paws as I move from one side to the other. It smells of fish, tar and old ropes, but I soon find a comfortable place in which to curl up and I feel peaceful and happy listening to the water lapping against the outside of our bowl.

"I perceive that you and your beast have made yourselves very much at home in MY boat!" growls a big man with a bushy black beard, bending over us and releasing a whiff of foul-smelling breath. "You must leave at once or I shall summon the *jandarma* from the castle and arrange to have you locked up."

In our haste to get ashore I rock the boat violently and fall into the water, but the Master grabs my collar and hauls me quickly back to land. It has been a rude awakening and I feel cold and surly as I shake myself vigorously, contriving to spray as much water as possible over the man with the beard. He uses a foul swear word and spits at the Master, but I grind my teeth emphatically which has the desired effect on him.

It is a still grey morning when we pause near the bridge to look back at the great castle of Rumeli Hisar in Europe, on the far side of the Bosphorus. We turn off the main road and strike inland, gathering our breakfast from the walnut and hazelnut trees along the way. We have reached the countryside at last - rather too damp, green and flat for our taste - but it is good to sniff the clean air and listen to the birds twittering in the bushes. We tramp towards the pale morning sun for an hour or more before meeting a man on a donkey leading a string of five camels. The senior camel looks very haughty, not at all like our beasts in the Taurus. He wears a handsome bridle - embroidered with blue beads, and he peers at me rather unpleasantly and refuses to acknowledge my friendly greetings. The Master becomes deeply engrossed in conversation with the man on the donkey, and it occurs to me that I might try a nip at one of the camel's rear legs!

"You must follow the sun," the man explains. "Go east, then south till it reaches its zenith; and after you have crossed the great highway running from Istanbul to Ankara - make sure that you cross with all speed - you will see the mountains ahead of you, mountains covered with pine trees and snow. Your bear will find plenty of honey in that region, and if you climb up to the small Lake of Abant you will discover a hotel by the shore where a man with such a fine bear might expect to earn a good living. It is a place much frequented by the rich business men and American tourists from Ankara."

The Master thanks the man for all this useful information and offers him a plug of tobacco for his *narghile*. Because he is clearly a man of discernment who appreciates a handsome bear when he meets one, I decide not to bite his camel and we continue on our journey.

A few kilometres further south we pass through a region of flowering cherry trees; the pale pink blossom blows hither and thither on the wind, some of it settling in the thick fur that covers my head and shoulders.

"Thou hast the appearance of a bride decked out with all that blossom!" laughs the Master, clutching his ribs.

I claw at the little flowers but they cling like leeches, so I jump up and down shaking my head vigorously and growling at the Master when he laughs louder than ever. We spend two days in that soft landscape of fruit and nut trees where there is plenty to eat, but the roots are soft and mushy and I develop a strong desire to clamp my teeth on something solid.

We reach the great highway about mid-morning on the third day, and scuttle across it with all haste to avoid the three roaring lines of devils on wheels, each determined to get ahead of the one beside him. Gassy fumes rush up our nostrils and we move swiftly away down a side road, thankful to have escaped unharmed.

An hour or two later we come to a big lake called Sapanca, with a pretty *lokanta* surrounded by poplar trees dipping its feet into the water. The Master urges me to dance as the chef is standing at the back door smoking a cigarette. I am very tired and do not wish to exert myself; but also very hungry, so I shuffle around on my hind legs and try to make the man smile.

He seems a serious type of chef, not much inclined for entertainment; but he has a kind face and soon perceives that we are tired and hungry. Clearly it is unthinkable for him to turn strangers away without sustenance, so he forages around in his kitchen and returns with some lemon tea and spiced meatballs for the Master and a big bowl of Harvest Crunch with honey and milk for me. We smack our lips with pleasure at such a tasty meal, and when the chef comes over to see how we are getting along the Master says; "May Allah give strength to your hands, *Effendi,* for truly you are a great chef!"

Our host grins happily -

perhaps his clients seldom bother to praise him - and he goes indoors again and fills a plastic bag with some nice morsels for our journey. The Master attempts to make him a present of his last plugs of tobacco but the chef firmly refuses to accept it. They shake hands and he expresses a wish that Allah will watch over us on the way to our homeland.

My paws have become soft during our long stay in the big city where there were no sharp rocks nor rough paths strewn with brambles and knife-edged stones. I look at the Master's feet and notice that his shoes, which were only cheap ones to begin with, are torn and painful to his toes. He perceives the train of my thoughts and says; "Let us plunge our feet in the lake, Boris. It is a warm afternoon and we shall feel much refreshed."

We are some distance from the *lokanta* by this time, so we paddle around in the cold water without fear of creating a spectacle. I try leaping up and down in order to splash the Master, but he scoops up cupfuls of water with his hands and throws them over my head. In the middle of this game we become aware of a small lorry, painted blue, yellow and red, containing some farm-workers who seem delighted with our antics. The lorry draws to a halt and the driver and his companions jump down to watch us from the road. This embarrasses the Master who stops throwing water over me, and we paddle demurely back to the beach.

"Where are you going, my brother? asks the driver. "Perhaps we can give you a lift."

"We are going to the mountains, *Effendi*," replies the Master; "but our feet are dripping wet."

"It does not matter. Jump in here with us!" shout the young men from the back, and the girls also give us friendly smiles and *Hoş geldiniz* (Welcome)."

The lorry coughs and splutters, then the engine roars into life and I can see Lake Sapanca flashing past us as we trundle along the road towards the mountains. What a grand sensation it is! No more slogging, hour after hour, on four weary paws with the sun beating down on our heads. I feel like a king bear squatting beside these warmhearted people, with the landscape slipping by with the speed of lightning. I would be very happy to remain in this lorry till we reach our final destination - despite the harsh words I may have uttered about the monsters crossing the Bosphorus Bridge.

An hour or so later, however, the driver swings round and says to the Master, "I will drop you at the next cross-roads as we are going to Zonguldak on the Black Sea coast."

All too soon we grind to a halt and the Master jumps out and holds out his arms to help me down. I wedge myself firmly between some packing-cases and make it quite clear that I do not wish to move; but this makes the farm-workers roar with laughter and a girl puts an arm round my neck and kisses me on the left ear! Nothing like this has ever happened to me before but, all too soon, alas, it is over. And the Master and I are limping along the dusty road once more, waving to our new friends until their beautiful carriage fades away in a cloud of dust.

It was fortunate that we had such happy experiences on the shores of Lake Sapanca, because our luck turned as soon as we came within sight of the mountains. In the first place they are the Köruğlu Mountains, not our own mountains at all, although we were not to know this until many days had passed. The Master, who never went to school, thought the Taurus Mountains were the only ones in Turkey; those mighty snow-capped giants where he would instantly feel at home and be able to find his tribe. With this idea fixed in his mind, he sets off at a brisk pace with a gleam in his eye, while I do my best to keep up with him despite my sore paws.

We tramp and scramble and climb for days on end, and each day it grows colder and wetter with silent snow-flakes continually falling out of a leaden sky. There are dark dripping pine-trees, whichever way you look, and it is hard to get a clear vista of the mountain peaks from the depths of this dismal forest.

The words of the camel man come back to us on the fourth day. By that time we are very very hungry (where is all that honey he mentioned, I muse?) and shivering cold. Even my thick pelt is not enough to keep us warm at night, and the Master has developed a bad cold and cough, and has eaten hardly enough to sustain a field-mouse for some days.

"Let us search for that hotel on a lake," he says to me in a hoarse voice. "Perhaps our troubles will grow less if we can earn a few good meals and sleep in a warm dry place."

A short while later we meet some forestry-workers who direct us along the steep road to Lake Abant. Towards evening we begin to descend and see a shining white lake through a clearing in the trees. Their dark trunks lean outwards at this place, and they have sharp twig branches pointing at the frozen lake as if to say; "Here is your dreampool at last, the famous spot where all the fat trout are lurking just beneath the surface..."

Drooping grasses emerge from the thin ice near the shore and already a few crocuses are pushing their yellow and purple heads through the snow. It looks a nice place and the Master sits down on a rustic bench while I squat beside him so that we can contemplate the far shore and the pine-clad hills beyond.

"Get moving, you two!" growls a harsh voice behind us. "These are the grounds of a 3-star hotel, and His Excellency, the Proprietor, never tolerates vagabonds in his domain."

The large man wearing a green uniform fixes us with a contemptuous stare and spits in our direction, the globule of saliva only just missing my Master's torn shoes. I follow his gaze and observe someone I can hardly recognize sitting beside me: his face is gaunt and unshaven, his eyes red with fever and his thin city clothes hang on him in tatters, like those inhabited by a scarecrow.

At that moment a sudden and overwhelming desire to kill this rude

stranger wells up inside me, and the first rumblings of his death-knell escape from my throat.

But my Master, who understands every sound that I utter, puts a gentle hand on my shoulder and says, "Come, little brother; do not enrage thyself for no good would come of it. We will wander on a little further to some other place where we may find a warmer welcome."

Mature bears, I need not tell you, do not burst into tears; but I felt so frustrated, embittered and saddened for the sake of my poor Master that it was all I could do to restrain my emotions and follow him obediently.

We plod on and on along the shores of this inhospitable lake, and I can hear wolves howling in the distance as the shades of night enclose us. The fur on my back begins to bristle as I recall the savage brutes that always hunted in large packs in the Taurus Mountains.

"Look, Boris. There is a cave on the side of that hill. Let us climb up there for we may find shelter, and I am near the end of my tether."

The Master turns left up a slippery track in the snow, and at last we reach the cave which has a sandy floor and a big rock that partially conceals the entrance. He crawls inside, gives a deep sigh of weariness, then lies on his back. I ferret around under the snow to find some roots for my supper - my meals have been of the coarsest and simplest variety ever since we left Lake Sapanca. Afterwards I lean against the rock and listen to the wolves howling and my Master coughing and breathing harshly inside the cave.

"He must be cold and hungry," I ponder; "why don't I find him something nice to eat?"

Then a jewel of an idea occurs to me and I move cautiously away from the cave so that he will not perceive my absence, and back down

Artist: Abigail Webster

the hill to the shores of the lake. I crouch under a tree, the branches of which project over the thin ice, and settle down to wait patiently; my eyes are riveted to a smooth patch of ice in front of me and my tense breath floats upwards into the still night air. A few minutes later my patience is rewarded for a big fish appears, waving its forked tail to and fro as it hunts for its supper close to the bank.

I dare not pause to think, so I leap forward and crash through the ice into the freezing lake. But Allah must have been watching me and, realizing the extreme importance of my task, arranged for the startled fish to leap out of the water and descend on dry land. I rapidly put an end to its flapping convulsions with a sharp smack of my right fore-paw, then grasp it between my teeth and scramble up the hill with all haste.

A red glow comes from the entrance to our cave, and I can see the Master crouching over a small fire that he is feeding with pine cones. A look of intense relief and joy spreads across his face as he watches me approach.

"Praise be to Allah that thou art safe, little brother!" he exclaims. "I thought thou hadst wandered off and been devoured by the wolves. And where didst thou find that heavensent fish?"

Once again, I longed for the power of human speech to describe - without undue modesty - the splendour and subtlety of my fishing exploit. But the best reward of all is to watch the expression on the Master's face as he prepares the fish and cooks it with deep concentration over the little fire, then lays it on a bed of pine needles and divides it exactly down the middle - half for me and half for himself.

It has begun to snow again; big silent flakes that cover us in a white mantle as we sit close together by the dying embers of the fire eating our first trout.

I prefer to draw a curtain over the next few days: the cold and misery, the fact that we were lost, frightened and always hungry; and my growing conviction that my Master would soon die. Some primitive instinct drew us slowly out of those gruesome mountains - moving north with our backs to the midday sun, then down and down till we came to a broad clearing at the foot of the hills. It was a place of stony red earth and scrubby grass, with a wind-shield of tall reeds held together by horizontal branches in the middle of it and, nestling among the reeds, a black goat-hair tent.

I have a sudden premonition that we have reached a crucial moment in our lives - a matter of life or death, with our lives hanging on a slender thread. Much depends on the next few minutes... and on me, in particular. A small boy is standing outside the tent watching us with interest. I rise on to my rear paws, clap my front ones above my head and begin to dance. All the strength has drained out of my bones these last few days and it is very hard to keep my balance, especially as the Master is too weak to play his tambourine and urge me forward. Never mind, the little boy is clearly entranced and he moves gingerly towards us, his expression a mixture of fear and delight.

I become intensely aware of what is happening around me as I struggle to do a polka. The Master, for instance, has slumped down on the ground behind me, his head hanging to one side so that it rests on a mound of earth; the little boy, who has big holes in his trousers and socks and wears no shoes, turns round to beckon to a man who has just emerged from the tent.

My back legs gradually give way and, a moment later, I collapse on to the hard red earth beside my Master - no better than a shabby bundle of fur fit for the dust-cart.

*   *   *   *

Chapter IV

M. S. Zonguldak

(Ben's Story)

The dinner-gong clanged at seven o'clock sharp, and Ma has just made a grand entrance into the dining-saloon wearing her new blue and gold evening-dress. Pa looked like a hedgehog faced with a plate of pilchards when he first set eyes on it!

"Where and when did you buy that creation?" he wanted to know; "and exactly how much did it cost?"

Pa never cares for new things that he cannot add to a funny list he keeps, headed 'Prudent Expenditure' - never mind who has paid for them. He is a solisistor, or some such word, and Ma is always telling people what an important man he is; senior partner of the best-known legal firm in Boringham, she says. He is very kind and helpful to lots of people and he never forgets my birthday; also he gives Ma and me lovely presents for Christmas. But when it's a question of one of us spending some money, even if it's our own, he turns very peculiar and his forehead gets all puckered up like a pug dog's, because the thoughts buzzing round inside his brain seem to hurt him. Now Ma is not like that at all. She loves to spend money and Pa says that it runs through her fingers like water through a sieve.

Other years, we have always spent our holidays in a cottage that Pa rents near the beach at Chudleigh Tiverton.

"The Devonshire air and scenery is quite delightful," I overheard him telling our next-door neighbour one day; "and it's so much easier for my wife. No embarrassment over the boy such as one might expect in a hotel, d'you see what I mean?"

She saw quite clearly, she told him, and praised him for being such a considerate man. But Ma, I think, looks at it from a different point of view as she realizes that Pa has never accepted the fact that I am 'different' from other people's children, although there is nothing they can do to alter me.

Ma and I had grown to hate those boring summer holidays in the West Country. The dripping country lanes packed with bad-tempered motorists; the dismal cottage where she had to work harder than at home, as the Hoover was always broken and the water never ran hot enough to wash the plates properly; the horrid food in local cafés that smelt of vinegar and stale frying-fat; and the sight of me with my nose pressed against the dirty window-panes as the rain swept in from the Channel.

Last winter, however, Aunt Agnes, who was Ma's favourite aunt, died and left her a very nice legacy - £2,000 - with an unusual request attached to it. Ma showed it to me as she knew that she could trust me not to say a word to Pa. Aunt Agnes particularly wished, she wrote in her will, that her niece should spend this money on a holiday of her own choosing, and a few frivolities with which to brighten her life; nothing useful, worthy or dull, she had added, underlining those three words in heavy black ink. Making sure that she concealed this special request from my father, Ma set about the task of persuading him to arrange a totally different type of holiday, to be paid for by her late aunt.

She brought home lots of exciting travel brochures, mentioned his brilliance as a classical scholar at university, read out tempting bits from his student-day travel books about the old ruins in Asia Minor and hinted that the Turks, being strict Muslims, had a reputation for kindness to people who were 'different', like me. By her clever way of handling things, she soon had Pa believing that it was he himself who had first thought of this marvellous idea of visiting ancient Byzantium, followed by a voyage around the coast on a Turkish ship. I was bursting with excitement as I looked at the lovely beach scenes shown in the brochures, and an unusual warmth seemed to flow out of Pa when he realized the enormous pleasure that he was proposing to give his family!

The dining-saloon is already full of people and many of them swing round to look at Ma as she advances in her new dress, nodding to right and left as if she were a princess! Even I peer at her with round eyes, and wish that someone would notice my new T-shirt. Pa clearly feels proud, but rather surprised, that such a plain little woman, as I've heard him describe her to his friends, should make such a favourable impression on the other passengers.

"We must order something special to celebrate the occasion!" he announces cheerfully, after we have been introduced to the four other people sharing our table. "Steward, bring me a bottle of champagne."

The steward, who has glossy black hair and rather sad brown eyes, surrounded by fierce eyebrows and a bristling moustache, spreads out his hands in a gesture of regret and says "Yok!"

"Yok! What's the stupid fellow talking about?" Pa demands sharply. "Do any of you good people understand this lingo?"

A small man who resembles a robin and has just begun to hum some classical music says, "Yes; you'll often hear that word in Turkey and its literal translation is 'there is not'; but it's a forceful little word that can be used to counter any tiresome requests or terminate tedious conversations! Why not try some of the local wine? It's really very drinkable."

Pa glares at the steward who is hanging around uncomfortably behind our chairs and orders a bottle of red wine, pronouncing each word loud and clear as though he were talking to a child from the nursery school. This causes some of the passengers at neighbouring tables to titter.

The man sitting opposite me - a tall man with freckles and very blue eyes with a twinkle in them - suddenly leans forward and says to me; "Are you a racing driver? I notice you're wearing a Grand Prix shirt with Ferraris whizzing across it!"

This idea really pleases me as I try to imagine myself hunched over a driving-wheel, my right foot jammed hard down on the accelerator and the trees and hedges flashing past me with the speed of lightning. I gurgle with excitement, but soon come back to earth with a nasty bang when I notice that Ma is wearing her 'I-have-something-private-to-reveal-to-you' expression, as she leans towards the small dark woman on her left. I suffer terribly every time this happens, as I know exactly what she is about to whisper:

"Yes, that's my son sitting there and he's really a quite remarkable child considering everything. You see, he suffered brain damage as a baby due to encephalitis which he developed after his vaccination. Of course it was one chance in a million, and it never occurred to us at the time or we'd never have had him done. But, inspite of all that, he's a wage earner and brings home £60 a week, can you imagine it?"

She pauses to draw breath and see what effect this revelation is having on her neighbour, but the dark woman's attention has wandered as she watches the handsome second mate who is about to leave the dining-saloon. Her husband, meanwhile, hums a waltz tune while he peers out of the nearest porthole.

"Why does she have to tell all that to strangers?" I ask myself miserably, fingering my forehead to make sure that my damaged brain is still inside my skull. "I don't FEEL any different to other people. I know I'm not clever like Pa, and can't do sums nor speak foreign languages, and the girls never want to play games with me. But I can do lots of other things, some of them even better than Ma herself." My eyes come to rest on a table in the middle of the dining-saloon where four Turkish people are seated, two men and two women. The men are dressed in ordinary suits and look like bank managers or lawyers, but their wives are wearing white veils - *Yaşmaks*, Ma says they are called, and they can be used to conceal their faces whenever required. The remainder of their costumes consist of round-necked blouses and long skirts made of some striped woollen material. In the way that people sometimes react to the gaze of a distant stranger, one of the women slowly raises her eyes and looks straight into mine for a long moment. I see a face I shall never forget - like an angel must look, she seems so grave and beautiful; and when she smiles at me it is like the rising of the sun from behind a bank of dark clouds.

*   *   *   *

"Hurry up and finish your pudding, Ben," Pa nudges my arm. "The ship's beginning to slow down which means we're coming into the Dardanelles, and we'll pop out on deck to see what's going on."

We have just devoured three courses: yokes of egg floating in meat soup, a rice dish full of pine nuts, currants and onions served with a salad of something called pureed aubergines; and, finally, baklava, that delicious pudding. The other people at our table have become quite talkative, and both Pa and I have started to make friends with the tall man with a twinkle - well, he was the first person to notice my new T-shirt, wasn't he? I have even exchanged a quick smile with this man's wife who does not look at all fierce, although it's hard to be sure as her head was buried in a Turkish dictionary for much of the meal. Now, however, she is having a serious conversation with Ma - not about me, thank goodness, but about some children who went to sea in a Thames sailing-barge. My ears are as sharp as a ferret's, and I have inherited Ma's habit of eavesdropping whenever there is something interesting to listen to.

Pa and I go out on the lower deck and stand by the rail gazing at the lights of Chanak. The ship has almost come to a standstill, and a brilliant lamp is flashing at us from the signal station while a pilot-boat puts out from the shore.

"This strip of water was called the Hellespont in ancient days," Pa tells me; "and it was over there that Xerxes, the Persian king, sat on his throne more than two thousand years ago. You see, he was unable to get across this narrow channel because the bridges he had ordered to be built for the passage of his mighty army had all been destroyed by a violent tempest."

Pa points towards the wooded shore that lies dark and mysterious beyond the lights of the signal station. "He was terribly angry, being in a fearful hurry to march westwards and punish the

Greeks, so he ordered the waters of the Hellespont to be lashed three hundred times and all his bridge engineers to be beheaded!"

"What a funny thing to do!" I exclaim, gazing at Pa with astonishment. But my attention soon begins to wander as I notice the black water churning to silver and gold around the pilot-boat, with a marvellous splodge of emerald, the reflection of one of its lights, quivering in the darkness below me.

I like it when Pa tells me these strange stories of long ago, but the past and future are words without meaning to me in a general sense, as I am much more interested in the immediate present - the sounds, colours and smells around me and the curious vibes I pick up from certain people and animals. All these matters I find extremely interesting, and really quite enough with which to fill my brain.

Presently Ma comes out on deck wearing a warm wrap over her beautiful new dress, and we all drink coffee under the stars outside the upper deck bar, sharing our table with an elderly judge from London. Pa, who is facing the north shore of the Dardanelles, begins to give us a lecture about the Gallipoli campaign during the First World War. I soon stop listening and think, instead, about some of the new people I have met today, dividing them into two groups: the ones I like and the ones I don't. Usually I place far more people in the first category, and today has been no exception. I specially liked the man who sang, pouring out his heart to the birds in the sky; also Mustafa, our cabin steward, and the man with twinkling blue eyes at our dinner-table who seems to understand things and does not ask me difficult questions; and I must not forget the Turkish lady with the angel's face. On the other hand I did not particularly care for the judge's wife - the one who objected to my singer - nor the little dark woman at our table. "Call me Dorothy," she had twittered to Ma at the end of our meal, at the same time glancing at me with eyes full of poisoned darts.

Pa has warmed to his subject by this time, and is waving a dripping coffee-spoon around agressively while he lines up our cups as if he were a general pointing out the enemy's reinforcements. He and the judge are having a lovely time telling each other how they would have won the battle, so Ma begins to day-dream and I can tell from her expression that she is somewhere very far away.

I get up quietly and creep on silent toes into the shadows, then climb a steep ladder to the top deck. It is quite deserted up here and I sit down in a deck-chair and gaze at the sky. The moon is shining through some fast-flying clouds that look like a big white sea-bird trying to escape from some terrible danger. The ship throbs beneath me as the lights of Chanak fade into the night; and the masts become living creatures waving their thin arms across the brilliant starry sky. I think of the bear, and remember that Pa once mentioned a cluster of stars called the Great Bear. I lie back in my chair and try to pick out those bearlike stars, but my glasses will keep misting over which makes it very difficult to keep the stars apart.

Away to the north lies the great cemetery where Pa told me that thousands of soldiers were buried who died on the battlefields at Gallipoli. But the M.S. *Zonguldak* steams steadily west towards a bright flashing lighthouse and the sea full of dark mysterious islands beyond the Dardanelles.

*   *   *   *

During the night we passed a number of places that I would have liked to see: Cape Baba, for instance, with an old fortress on its summit, filled with soldiers and machine-guns; also a channel running between the Greek island of Mytiléne and the Turkish coast, where the patrol-boats from each country lurk in small coves ready to pounce on smugglers or secret agents. Dorothy's husband, the man who hums such nice tunes, told us all about these places at breakfast. I suppose he spends all night on deck watching out for them.

Dorothy has been staring at me for some while and suddenly she leans forward and says, "I hear you've got bears on the brain!" Then she begins to titter.

This upsets me very much as it means that Ma (who has coloured up and won't meet my eyes) has been telling this horrible woman about my adventure in the park in Istanbul. I feel like spitting at both of them, for they are like swine compared with that man and his bear.

"Come out on deck with me, Ben," Pa calls from the door - he finished his breakfast earlier. "The ship is just approaching Izmir."

We stroll around the deck together and watch the little pilotboat racing towards our ship, and the pilot leaping on to the rope ladder which some sailors have let down for him. I pause near the back end (Pa calls it the stern-deck) to look at the coils of thick orange rope waiting to tie us to the shore, and the white frothy water rushing past us...

"Come on, Ben! You're missing the best part," Pa calls out from further along the deck. "We're just coming alongside the quay."

I join him at the same moment that Dorothy appears on deck and sidles up to him on the other side.

"There are all our new passengers waiting to join the ship," she tells Pa, pointing to a group of people standing together outside the custom-house." They've been visiting some of the ancient sites like Ephesus and Pergamum, and the purser tells me that one of them is a famous scientist from Bavaria, a Professor Lindenbaum, who is causing a sensation in the field of brain surgery in western Europe."

Her eyes are ice-blue and hard, and they never seem to blink when she tells you something important and waits with parted lips to see what effect it will have. Why does she hate me so much, I ask myself?

The new passengers move towards the gangway, followed by some Turkish porters carrying their luggage. I study them closely and my eyes fasten on a fat man with a puffy white face who has fingers like newborn piglets that are never at rest. They seem to be quarrelling with one another as they beat a tattoo on the gangway rail, and now and then they fly upwards to scratch his bald pink head, leaving nasty red marks behind them.

The passengers are welcomed aboard by the purser who takes them below to see their cabins. Meanwhile the rest of us leave the ship. I feel confused and miserable, until the Turkish lady with the white veil comes up behind me and squeezes my arm in a friendly way. I rise into the air on a magic carpet, and while I'm up there I catch sight of the singer coming down the gangway, his arms outstretched like the wings of a seagull as he begins to sing. Then I know that life is beautiful, even if there are dark shadows here and there.

*   *   *   *

"Of the ancient Greek cities on the coast of Asia Minor, Izmir (or Smyrna, as it was formerly called) is the only one that has survived to this present day."

Pa is lecturing to a captive audience who cannot easily escape from him as they are all waiting for the same coach to take them to see the Roman Agora and the Museum of Archaeology. The judge and his wife and Dorothy and her husband are among them, but the nice tall man from our table gives me a wink as he and his wife cross the road to watch some white ducks swimming around on a pond on the other side. Pa looks bristly because his lecture is not being listened to by everyone, but Ma becomes quite envious when she sees this couple accepting a lift in a strange Turkish car

to go to the shopping bazaar.

She and I try to behave ourselves plodding round the Agora, being told exactly what to look at by a very bossy guide. But when we reach the museum she has had enough, and Pa seems quite glad to get rid of us; perhaps he wants to have a private talk with Dorothy.

We soon find our way to an old mosque, and beyond it a rabbit-warren of little streets covered with vine leaves to keep them cool when the sun is overhead. It is a magic place, this rabbit-warren, for there are hundreds of tiny shops and all the ones selling the same goods are clustered together. There are the carpet weavers and leather sandal-makers, the copper-smiths who sell marvellous trays and coffee-pots, and in another part of the bazaar you can find small enamel boxes painted with scenes of castles and sultans wearing turbans riding on donkeys, and strings of camels with brilliant-coloured saddle-bags. But the part that Ma and I love the best is the gold and silver bazaar where all kinds of jewelry glitters in the shafts of sunlight that creep through the vine-leaf roof.

Ma sees a bracelet that really takes her fancy so, muttering something about "dear Aunt Agnes", then "promise me you won't say a word to your father", she leads me into this little shop. We are invited to sit down on round leather seats, and the shopkeeper claps his hands and orders a boy to fetch us cups of tea. I feel as if I were a prince in one of those stories from the "Arabian Nights" as I sit here sipping my tea out of a tiny cup while Ma bargains with the shop-keeper.

Then the most wonderful thing happens: the two Turkish gentlemen from our ship with their veiled ladies come into the shop and greet us with big smiles. My special lady examines a shining blue stone with a black spot in the middle of it, set in gold with a tiny golden ring attached to it. The blue is the colour of a peacock's feathers, as blue as the sky above us... I stand there admiring it and she looks at me then whispers something to her husband - she cannot speak any English. He listens to her and smiles, then turning to Ma addresses her very politely:

"It would give my wife great pleasure," he says, "if your son would accept a small gift from us? It is something that many people in Turkey wear to bring them good luck and keep away the evil spirits."

Ma looks rather surprised, but she cannot very well say "no" as she is just about to buy herself an expensive bracelet; and when she sees how starry-eyed I look she jumps up and gives the lady a kiss on both cheeks. The shop-keeper sends for more tea, and we are all as happy as bees in a hive full of honey!

*   *   *   *

Later that afternoon Ma and I walk through a park that is full of people sitting under big dark trees gazing at a lake, and men selling pink and mauve balloons. She buys me a balloon and we play with it till the breeze blows it over the lake, then some men wade into the water in their shoes and socks to chase it and everyone begins to laugh; but it rises higher and higher till it is carried away over the minarets of a distant mosque, far away into the sky.

I like it here and could stay all day, but we have to meet Pa for dinner at a restaurant on the end of a pier.

We arrive there exactly at seven, out of breath from running so as not to keep Pa waiting; but he is here already, seated at a table on one side of the pier, tapping impatiently on his guide-book with a fork. The west wind blows hard, causing white horses to gallop into the bay and toss spray over his shoes from time to time. It is a lovely place, like the deck of a ship, and Ma and I are bursting with things to tell him about the balloon chase and the present I was given in the bazaar and we take one look at his face and the words die in our throats. Pa looks edgy and full of some important business of his own that he wants to discuss with Ma, immediately - but not in front of me.

That is something I really hate - this rude habit some grown-up people have (and that includes Ma) of wanting to talk about me in private. Why can't they do it late at night, or when I'm not around to be got rid of in such a hurtful way? I know that my words come pouring out in a funny way, but I can understand, remember and, above all, feel things just as deeply as any of them.

"See if you can buy me an English newspaper at that kiosk across the road, will you, Jack?" And Pa hands me some Turkish money.

There is no chance of my hiding somewhere on the pier so that I can eavesdrop, so I trudge angrily across the road, hating Pa with all my guts. When I return with the newspaper and change Ma looks quite different from the person who played balloons with me in the park; she looks strung up and miserable, as if she might suddenly burst into tears. I begin to wonder if Pa has discovered her new bracelet? But no, there is something else on their minds that is way beyond my simple understanding.

We eat our dinner in silence, without pleasure; and I feel sorry for the waiter who tries so hard to make us enjoy his food. I want to say something nice to him to make up for our behaviour but what can I say?

Back aboard M.S. *Zonguldak* the gangway is lifted at nine o'clock and the ship's belly begins to rumble for going to sea. The evening sun is lurking behind a dark bank of clouds and the wind has suddenly dropped. But there is no magic in the air this evening, and I know that the stars will not twinkle in the night sky. Never mind, I have my beautiful blue bead to bring me luck and I am wearing it on a chain round my neck so that I shall never lose it.

Chapter V
The Emperor Bear
(Boris's Story)

"Köroğlu was a bandit - a great hero, mind you - who lived in this region four hundred years ago," explains Yakup; "and it was in his honour that these mountains received their name." We are seated round a glowing fire of pine logs and goat's dung: the Master, Yakup and his family and I. Every evening their little ass, Sasha, - I find her a very modest and charming companion - comes clip-clopping down the mountain track laden with firewood and the boy, Mehmet, runs along behind her. And, later on, we sit round this beautiful fire with the cooking-pot slung from a tripod, bubbling away in our midst; and Yakup, with the manners of a perfect host, always urges my Master to take the warmest seat.

What splendid friends we have found in this poor *Yörük* family. They built us a shelter of pine branches next to their tent, and made soft beds of pine needles covered with sheep's wool for the Master and me to lie on; then Fatma prepared a concoction of mountain herbs to cure the Master's fever, and she brought us bowls of nourishing soup and home-baked bread, the slices spread thick with Mengen cheese or pine honey (for me) to restore our strength. And, yesterday, Mehmet brought me a little slice of hazelnut candy to round off my supper. Allah alone knows how much these people must have starved themselves to nurse us back to health. Why, even little Sasha insisted on my sharing her nose-bag this evening; she said she had no appetite, but I find it difficult to believe this considering how hard she has to work.

"Tell me about this Köroğlu?" the Master asks. "He must indeed have been a great man to have a range of mountains named after him."

"Well, Köroğlu, as you know, means 'son of the blind man'," continues Yakup. "His father was a groom serving the Lord of Bolu, and he was ordered to select a gift horse from among the herd of a neighbouring Bey. Instead of choosing a fine animal of noble ancestry, he picked a lean and crippled colt, and this so enraged his master that he had the groom's eyes put out. Köroğlu vowed revenge and, with the help of the colt, now grown into a magic grey horse called Kirat, he spent the rest of his life robbing fat merchants and lords of the provinces on their journeys across the mountain passes. He had soon assembled a band of 500 warriors and his fame spread far and wide, from Istanbul in the west to Armenia in the east."

"What a fantastic story," murmurs the Master, his eyes half closed as a spiral of smoke rises from his *narghile* and drifts upwards into the cold night air. "But was it just an ancient legend, d'you suppose, or did this man really exist?"

"Of course he really existed!" declares little Mehmet, with a fierce gleam in his eyes. "And there are one or two like him, even today." His father smiles at the boy through the thin veil of smoke and says quietly; "I was once told by a *Yörük* from the south who had passed through Ankara, that there is a big building in that city called a museum; anyone may enter this place, so he wandered around until he came to a room in which there were some letters written by the Governor of Ankara about 1590, demanding Köroğlu's immediate arrest!"

*   *   *   *

The rising sun is sending long golden beams through the slits in our roof of pine branches, and I can see a million rainbow-coloured specks dancing up and down. I have just awoken from a beautiful dream: I was standing beside a sky-blue lake in the springtime, with my paws submerged in a carpet of flowers; and there were little groups of fir trees, standing together stiff and straight as soldiers, along the crests of the distant hills. A mighty snow-clad mountain rose up behind them - a mountain like the Ala Dağ where I was born. And, suddenly, a familiar scent came wafting across the lake and my nostrils began to twitch with excitement... then it all faded away and here I am, stretching my limbs luxuriously and scratching my armpits. I find this restful life suits me to perfection.

"Art thou awake, little brother?" the Master's voice breaks through my reflections. "Because we must leave this haven of peace. We have been the guests of these wonderful people, and they have certainly saved our lives and restored us to health so that we may continue our journey. But first I have some ideas that I will share with thee during our walk into town.

"Yakup and his family have risen early and taken Sasha with them into the hills, to gather nuts and firewood and find fresh pasture for their goats. They told us last evening that they might not be back till late, so the Master pulls me briskly out of bed and brushes my fur, then we set off at a fast pace down the track to Bolu.

It is market day in the city, and he tells me what I must do so that we can repay our good friends in some small measure. There are no tourists in this area, but I soon succeed in collecting a big crowd of country people around me in the market-place. The Master begins to beat an exciting rhythm on his tambourine and I dance and dance; then I seize the tambourine from him and, holding it upside-down, I waltz around our audience, offering it to them between my two front paws. Soon the kuruş begin to patter into it like summer rain and when it is nearly full, we retire to a quiet corner to count our earnings.

They are greater than we had dared to hope, even exceeding a good day in Istanbul; so the Master leads me to the shopping quarter and buys me some bananas to eat while he is doing the other shopping. He attaches my lead to a lamp-post in a public garden, and I squat on my haunches and think about Sasha and how much I shall miss her.

After a long while he returns laden with packages, and gives me a big morsel of chocolate and hazelnut candy to sweeten my temper.

"I have bought presents for everyone," he announces. "A new axe and a sheepskin waistcoat for Yakup, a fine white *yasmak* and some material for a blouse for Fatma, a pair of smart trousers and shoes for little Mehmet and a blue bead necklace for Sasha! Dost thou think these gifts will bring pleasure, my Boris?"

He ruffles the fur behind my ears and I nod my head to please him; but my brain is full of worries for the future. How shall we manage on our own again, tramping on and on across this strange countryside? And how shall I survive without my little slave, Sasha, to look after my needs?

"Thou art a truly selfish bear!" laughs the Master, reading my thoughts. "Come, for we must hurry so that we can leave these parcels in the camp before Yakup returns, then he cannot refuse to accept them."

We are quite out of breath by the time we arrive at the clearing below the trees, not yet being very strong after our illness. The Master places his gifts inside the tent, then collects our few belongings from our cosy shelter and turns towards the dark forest behind us. I follow him sadly, and I can feel big tears welling up in my eyes as I take one last look over my shoulder at the lonely goat-hair tent.

We scramble through the thick undergrowth till we have put a good distance between ourselves and Yakup's camp; then we build a little fire beneath a rocky ledge and settle down to cook our supper of spiced meat-balls and potatoes, followed by large mouth-watering slices of *baklava* - the last of the Master's purchases from Bolu.

He is useless at saving money is the Master, I reflect; and I cannot help wondering what we shall have for dinner tomorrow night.

"Well, thou couldst always search for nuts and myrtle-berries and, perhaps, catch a few field-mice!" he suggests with a big grin on his face; just as though I had spoken my thoughts out loud in human language.

Then we hear the *muezzins* in Bolu calling the faithful to the mosques. I scoop out a hollow for myself beneath the ledge and curl up to go to sleep while the Master climbs on top of the rocks to watch the setting sun and say his prayers.

*   *   *   *

The next few days are warm happy days filled with the first whispers of springtime. There is still a mantle of snow over the distant mountain peaks, but the fat green buds are bursting open on the trees in the valleys and the birds are singing their hearts out all around us.

These Köroğlu Mountains look as dark and blue as a midnight sky - not at all like our mountains, as I remember them. But we are keeping close to the road this time so that we shall not get lost again; and moving east towards the rising sun, then a little south till midday, just as Yakup instructed us.

On the second day we pass through Gerede, a big town at the junction of the main road leading to Ankara. Many lorry-drivers pause to refresh themselves in this place, and we find them to be men of unusual intelligence and generosity, who greatly appreciate my talents. After Gerede, I forget my persistent worries about empty bellies as I know that our meals are assured for the next few days.

"Look at that dog on the far side of the road," says the Master, pointing to a large cream-coloured animal with a fine black muzzle. "Does he not remind thee of Albay, little brother?"

These pleasant thoughts are soon dispersed by the dog himself who bares his teeth and releases a fierce growl from his cavernous mouth, his tail curling over his back and his fur fluffed up ready to attack us. "Peace, thou foolish animal," shouts his master, a young shepherd with a flock of red-bellied sheep (this is not their natural colour, but that of the Anatolian earth in which they must have squatted). "Canst thou not tell the difference between an honest man with a fine bear and a villain from the big city?"

The dog snuffles round us, still deeply suspicious. I form the impression that he has never met a bear before! But his master's words please my Master so much that he greets the man with great politeness and invites him to share our supper. This makes me rather angry as I had been looking forward to our evening banquet all day long; and when I contemplate that huge dog and try to assess the possible size of his appetite, I am filled with the darkest forebodings. The Master ignores me as he knows my thoughts, and I dare not make them too obvious as we are to be the hosts.

The shepherd leads us to a little hut at the end of a pond filled with golden-brown reeds and tall grasses. I can hear innumerable frogs leaping about in the pond, and their loud croaking reminds me of the days when I was a young bear.

"It's because spring is in the air that they are making such a deafening noise," the dog confides to me in a friendly manner. He is running along beside me now, clearly wondering what my Master has in his haversack for supper.

We leave the sheep grazing outside and enter the hut which has a bunk along one wall, a wood-burning stove, a table in the middle and a chair on either side of it. A tiny window gives a charming view of the blue mountains reflected in the pond.

"What a very cosy den you have," I observe to the dog. After all, he has made the first overtures so I must not be too stand-offish.

Meanwhile my Master has unpacked all our food for the next few days and, spreading it out on the table, he divides it into four equal portions; he carefully conceals the fact that it is meant to last till we reach another big town where we can earn some more money.

The shepherd lights the stove which soon begins to crackle merrily; then he fills a big drinking-bowl with water for his dog and me to share, and puts a kettle on the stove to make tea for the Master and himself. Despite my earlier misgivings, we all have a fine supper and much interesting conversation, while the seeds of friendship are quickly sown between the two men.

"I must go home to my wife and children now," announces the shepherd, after he has washed the cups and plates and smoked his *narghile* for a while, sitting beside my Master on the steps of the hut. They look like brothers, watching the sheep through a haze of smoke and chatting about this and that.

"You and Boris are very welcome to spend the night here," he says, rising to go; "and I will ask my cousin, who drives a bus along this road from Gerede to Amasya, to give you a lift when he stops near here in the morning."

The full impact of this arrangement did not strike me until the following day as the dog was whispering something important in my ear at the same moment.

"If you go to the edge of the woods on the far side of the pond early tomorrow morning, you will find a meadow full of young rabbits and you might catch one for breakfast!"

I thank him warmly for sharing his secret with me. Next morning, just before sunrise, after a cosy night curled up in front of

the stove, I creep out of the hut and make my way through the trees to the meadow. The grass is glittering with dew and the frogs are still croaking gently, their love-song muted while they squat in the reeds watching the sun climb over the eastern mountains. The dog has not exaggerated for the whole place is alive with young rabbits; but how can a mature bear like me, who has worked himself to the bone in the big city, be expected to catch such lively animals? They sit there and laugh at me, then vanish into their burrows before I can get close enough to estimate the plumpness of their rumps.

"Boris! Come back at once." The Master's voice sounds harsh and impatient; perhaps he has been shouting for some while. "Where hast thou been, thou villainous bear?" he demands anxiously as I trot towards him. He grabs my collar and rushes me across the road.

A large bus is puffing and panting beside a bus shelter and the driver, who has been talking to our shepherd, says *"Merhaba!"* (Hello) to us and tells us to get aboard quickly. The bus is full of people and a child opens its mouth to bawl when it sees me climbing up the steps; then everyone begins to talk at once.

"Come and sit beside me, old fellow," invites a huge *jandarma*, squeezing his neighbours into a corner to make room for me and the Master.

The bus starts moving and a woman draws her *yasmak* closely round her face so that she cannot see me. The *jandarma* tickles my ribs and tells me not to pay any attention to these inferior types of people. Soon we gather speed and I become aware of the same tingling sensation in my veins as I experienced in the lorry that picked us up near Lake Sapanca. I become a royal bear once again, with the landscape rushing by and the dust-filled wind rippling through my fur. I love the whole human race who have invented these iron monsters so that I can travel gloriously between A and B. The bus stops at a number of towns: Çerkes, Kurşunlu, Ilgaz (where the *jandarma* and all the passengers for the Black Sea coast leave us); then Ozmancik, Gümüşhacıköy and Merzifon. The mountains ahead of us look taller and wilder as we move east, the trees sparser and more wind-swept and there are fewer shepherds by the roadside. The master and I descend at some of these stops to obey the calls of nature and give short performances outside the travellers' *lokantas*, so that our dinner for tonight is already assured; all the same, I wish I had charge of the Master's purse!

After a brief stop at Merzifon, we are climbing back into the bus for the final stage of our journey when a most objectionable man with his family behind him orders the driver to put us off. The driver who is, after all, the cousin of our friend the shepherd, replies that he has promised to take us as far as Amasya and he cannot break his word. Besides, he points out, we have caused no trouble and given much pleasure to some of his passengers.

The man spits angrily on the pavement and looks around for a *jandarma*, but there are none in sight. He decides, in the end, to hire a taxi for himself and his family. All the remaining passengers give a loud cheer, some spit out of the windows in his direction and one old lady extracts a pot of honey from her shopping-bag and, pressing it into the Master's haversack, says, "This is a little gift for your beautiful bear!"

The sun is low in the sky by the time the bus rumbles into the terminus in Amasya. After thanking the driver for his great kindness in carrying us for so many miles, the aster and I wander through the narrow streets, gaze at the famous mosques and the old Ottaman houses overhanging the River Yesilirmak, buy some *börek* (a flaky pastry filled with herbs and meat) and stuffed aubergines for our supper.

"The shepherd told me that Amasya is one of the loveliest cities in Anatolia," the Master says, as we lean on the bridge parapet watching the reddish-yellow water flow by beneath us. "But the people here are not accustomed to bears so we shall climb up to the citadel to spend the night, little brother."

I am more interested in where and

55

when we shall have our supper, but I know it is unlikely to happen before we have settled our sleeping quarters so I make no fuss about following him up a steep winding track with a rock wall on the inner side. He shows me some of the carved rock tombs of the ancient Pontic kings on our way up, and when we reach the citadel itself I feel as if I was standing on the roof of the world.

We spread out our food in a sheltered corner beneath one of the watch-towers and, later on, when we are full and satisfied, the Master lights his *narghile* and points to the sky.

"Look at that group of stars above us," he says; "they are known as the Great Bear, Boris, It will surely bring thee good fortune to sleep beneath that constellation tonight. And tomorrow is a turning point in our travels; we have now travelled far enough east, according to the directions Yakup gave me, and tomorrow we shall turn south, towards the Taurus Mountains at last."

*　　*　　*　　*

I awake with a premonition of something extraordinary about to happen; not, perhaps, today nor tomorrow, but certainly within the next few days. There is a pale yellow glow in the sky above the parapet, and I lie quite still and watch the swallows darting in and out of the ruined watch-tower. I wish I could fly like a swallow, high above the roof-tops in the city!

Already the *muezzins* are calling the faithful to prayer in the valley below us, so the Master turns towards the east to say his prayers while I watch the first pink fingers of dawn creeping across the soft grey sky. When he has finished we stand close together, observing the scene spread out like a map beneath my paws.

"Look at that beautiful green plain with the yellow river

flowing through it," he exclaims, pointing towards the south. "In ancient times that river was called the Iris, which meant 'Messenger of the Dawn'. That is the route we shall take today towards the great citadel at Tokat."

He then leans out over the parapet to show me some of the famous mosques. I preserve a polite expression, such as a student bear in the presence of a learned professor might assume; but my real interest lies in the sounds and smells drifting up from the town. I can hear a goat bell ringing, the clip-clop of a donkey's hooves which reminds me of Sasha, noisy car-horns and rumbling wagon wheels. The air is touched with frost and crystal clear, and the tantalizing smell of meat grilling on a charcoal stove makes my nostrils begin to twitch.

"Come, little bear, we must start on our journey," says the Master, perceiving the drift of my thoughts. "I will buy thee some breakfast down in the town."

We descend the rocky path and find a very nice *lokanta* called the Çiçek (Flower) Restaurant for breakfast. The Master orders two big helpings of *lahmacun pide* (flat bread with minced meat, onions and tomatoes), a cup of mountain tea for himself and a bowl of mineral water for me. That sort of extravagance is typical of the man; as soon as he has a few *kuruş* in his pocket, ordinary plain water is not good enough for me!

After our meal the waiter comes to the door to wave us goodbye.

"Allahasmarladik!" (Allah go with you) says the Master and *"Güle güle!"* (Smilingly smilingly) replies the waiter.

A few minutes later we are out on the open road again,

with little donkey carts rumbling past us and women wearing red garments smiling and waving to us from the seat behind their drivers.

The sun rises higher in the clear blue sky, the fruit trees are heavy with blossom and the fields emerald-green with corn on either side of the long straight road to the south. Sometimes we rest by the yellow river and I cool my paws in the fast-flowing stream. Then we eat some bread and honey (from the pot given me by the old lady). The hours pass quickly and there are plenty of nuts and fruit to add to the food we have brought from Amasya.

On the afternoon of the second day the Master observes that the sun is getting hotter and the fields of corn are few and far between. I notice that his shoes are falling apart and sweat is pouring down his face and neck. Oh foolish Master, why didst thou not buy some new shoes when we were rich, with money in our purse?

Ahead of us lies a landscape of reddish-brown hills and distant snow mountains, with not a human habitation in sight. My paws are becoming very sore and the Master's feet are dragging more and more, but the sight of those mountains draws him south like a magnet attracts an iron nail.

A few hours later we limp towards a lonely garage by the side of the road. 'Türkpetrol' it announces from a smart new signboard.

"*Iyi akşamlar!*" (Good evening!) the Master greets the man standing near the petrol pump. "Please can you tell me how far the Taurus Mountains are from here?"

The man clicks his tongue against the roof of his mouth and raises his eyes to the heavens. "Three or four hundred kilometres at least," he says, spreading out his hands in the manner of someone who would rather spare us the answer to such a question. "But please sit down and I will make you a cup of tea, for I can see that you and your companion are very hot and tired."

The garage-keeper goes into his little office to boil the kettle and he soon returns with a bottle of lemon eau-de-cologne with which he sprays the Master's head and hands to refresh him. Then he goes inside again to fetch a big drinking-bowl for me and two cups of tea for the Master and himself.

"This tea is more welcome than a pot of gold," declares the Master, smacking his lips with pleasure. "Will you do me the honour, *Effendi,* of sharing a few slices of bread and honey with me and my bear?"

There he goes again! I growl with frustration as I happen to know that he is offering this man the last of our victuals from Amasya, and now, I suppose, we shall begin to starve again. The Master frowns at me and, later on, when we have left the garage and the man who was very pleased to accept a slice of our bread and MY honey, he gives me a lecture on how to behave when a stranger has offered us hospitality.

We spend a rough cold night in a hollow beside the road. I have a distinct edge to my appetite next morning when we pass within sight of the town of Zile but the Master, who is still angry with me and, I suspect, has *kurus* left in his purse, refuses to stop there.

We trudge on and on towards the midday sun with the hard brown earth hot under my paws and the snow-capped mountains as far away as yesterday, and the day before. Then, quite suddenly, it all begins to happen... We have reached the outskirts of the little village of Resadiye where there are a great number of cars parked on either side of the road and swarms of men dressed in city suits, flitting hither and thither like chickens. Some of them are very bossy and smell strongly of perfume (after-shave lotion, some people call it), causing an irritation inside my nostrils.

"Get off the road, you idiot!" one man shouts at the Master. "Hurry and get behind that car, immediately."

My Master has a peaceful nature and he is less inclined to dispute an order than I would be. The first rumblings of a spectacular growl are building up inside my belly; I am also very hungry which brings the primitive side of my nature to the forefront.

"Peace, little brother," whispers the Master; "no good will come of it if thou behavest badly."

All the villagers have emerged from their houses to watch and two fat women peer at me from behind their *yasmaks*, cackling to one another in a way that does little to appease my anger.

"Here he comes, the great man himself!" whispers a goatherd standing near to us. And suddenly everyone begins to clap.

"Why is he so great?" asks my Master, also in a whisper.

"Well, he was a very brave leader in times gone by; also a fine politician. But, as you can see, he is well advanced in years now," explains our neighbour. "Today he has come back to visit his home village, and they tell me that nine sheep have been sacrificed in his honour."

I step forward into the road and see a short square-faced man with iron-grey hair, intelligent eyes, a big mouth and many wrinkles. A pair of the city men are supporting him, one on either side, and I have a strange premonition that he is rather sad and ill. This knowledge, together with the sound of clapping hands which always excites me, causes me to do something quite extraordinary - something that I would never have dared to contemplate had I not been so enthralled by the scene in front of me: I advance into the middle of the road and begin to dance the cha-cha!

"Get that bear off the road at once, d'you hear me!" roars one of the guards at my Master.

But the great man himself raises his right hand and says, "Let him be. Seldom have I seen such a splendid dancing bear!"

Thus encouraged, I dance to my heart's content and, although my Master's face has turned scarlet with embarrassment, he beats a steady rhythm on his tambourine so that I shall not falter in my steps. At the end of the dance the people follow the great man's lead; when he laughs and claps and stamps his feet for more, they do the same. So I dance a tango, a waltz and a rumba, and the thrill of having such a distinguished audience keeps me on my back paws for half an hour or more.

*   *   *   *

Before the great Leader leaves his old mother's home, he sends for my Master and has a private talk with him in the kitchen. The city men are not invited to join them, but I am left on guard in her garden. After a short while the two men emerge and I notice that mine looks quite different; it is hard for me to place a paw on the exact details of this difference, apart from the fact that he appears several centimetres taller than before and there are stars in his eyes that dazzle me when he turns towards me.

A short while later the great man gets into a large black limousine and departs in a cloud of dust towards the north. As soon as the waving cheering crowd has faded away, the Master draws me aside to share with me his astonishing news.

"In one hour's time, my wonderful bear, try to picture where we shall be?" He is shaking all over, as if with a fever, but before he has time to reveal the cause we hear the old lady calling us from her kitchen, telling us to step inside at once as she has prepared a meal for us.

I shall never forget the taste of that luncheon; it is like a beautiful dream come true! The young lamb cooked to perfection over a charcoal grill, accompanied by roast potatoes and stuffed marrow, then plates of myrtleberry tart to follow. The old lady tends us as if my Master were a prince, but after the meal something very unexpected and disagreeable takes place: she brings a bowl of warm water, soap, a towel and a razor, so the Master washes his face and hands and has a shave; then he turns to me, observing that my appearance is a disgrace, and, seizing my collar he close-crops my whiskers and the lower part of my face as well! Never before have I been subjected to such an unpleasant experience, and I have just begun to growl in anticipation of what may follow when a man throws open the door and announces; "The pilot is ready!"

The Master hastily says *"Iyi günler"* to our kind hostess, and we follow this man through the village till we come to a long flat strip of open ground covered with sand and grass. There is a type of very large bird sitting in the middle of it, only it seems different from the eagles and vultures I have watched high up in the mountains, for it remains quite still and its belly is resting on wheels instead of feet with claws. The next moment we find ourselves climbing up a short staircase attached to its side, then the Master leads the way INSIDE its belly - just as though he did this sort of thing every day.

We are shown into small squatting positions by a young woman who greets me with a warm smile. The Master, who is still shaking like a windswept reed, allows himself to be strapped into his seat by this young female, but when she attempts to do the same to me I make it quite clear that I wish to remain free. A deep throbbing sensation causes the bird to shudder and run forwards; I just have time to notice the people squatting in front of us and feel the Master's hand gripping my shoulder so tightly that it hurts. Then the bird lets out a roar like a wounded bear and suddenly rises straight up into the sky!

This is certainly the most remarkable thing that has ever happened to me, and I feel like an emperor bear as I decide to stand on my seat so that I can see better, despite the Master's hands clutching at my fur. This bird has silver wings and it is high above the village now, soaring towards the mountains in the south. The young female returns with a tray of bottles and my Master accepts a glass of raki; most unusual behaviour, I tell myself. He drinks it in one gulp and, clearly, it makes him feel better as he lets go of my fur and settles down to sleep.

Some while later he wakes up with a start, rubs his eyes with amazement, then becomes quite talkative:

"It is thanks to the great Leader that we are travelling in this aeroplane," he tells me. "It brought him from Kayseri this morning and has to return there now, while he goes on to Samsun by car. But thou madest such a deep impression on him, my clever little bear, that he asked me where we were bound and suggested that we might care to use his plane to travel all the way to Cappadoceia!"

I am too excited by the clouds beneath our wings, the sight of rocky summits actually below our belly and the buzzing sensation in my ears, to pay much attention to what he is saying. But presently a man comes through a door from the beak of this bird and the Master whispers, "That's the co-pilot," and grips him by the sleeve.

"Please, *Effendi*, can you tell me the name of that mountain we are approaching?" he asks, pointing at an enormous snow giant, higher than all its brother mountains.

"Certainly," replies the co-pilot, with a friendly smile at me. "That is the mighty volcanic mountain, Erciyes Daği, the shining white guardian of the eastern end of the Taurus range. It is nearly 4,000 metres high and, after Ararat, it is one of the highest mountains in Turkey, I believe. We are coming down to land very shortly, so please will you make sure that your bear has his seat-belt fastened."

This time I put up no resistance. All the excitements of today have finally reduced me to the condition of a squeezed lemon.

"Didst thou hear what that man said, Boris?" The Master sounds quite breathless. "We have reached the Taurus Mountains at last! I will buy thee a beautiful blue bead necklace to bring thee good fortune, as soon as we land in Kayseri."

Chapter VI
The Dorian Peninsula
(Ben's Story)

The black horses with their glittering white manes have been galloping past my porthole all night long, and now the dawn is breaking and the horses are changing into waves - small blue-grey waves that run along the ship's side singing their special wave songs, over and over again.

The sky is pink and mauve - like Ma's moonstone pendant - and I can see a line of ink-black mountains between the sea and the sky; they are growing bigger and bigger every moment, so I must quickly get dressed and run up on deck.

Well, here I am, standing between my two friends, Mustafa, our cabin steward, and Mahmud, the singer. He is quiet and serious this morning, gazing at the sunrise as though it was a beautiful dream. Now that we are closer to the land the waves have gone to bed and there is a tiny island with two chimneys rising from it, black in the path of the sun. The deck-rail is wet with dew and I can smell something wonderful in the air...

"Pine trees and rosemary," murmurs Mustafa, seeing the way my nose is twitching. "Do you see a village below the mountains?" he asks me. "That is Datça, the place where *Zonguldak* drops anchor."

He bends down and pretends to pick up an imaginary object that is very heavy, staggers to the ship's rail and throws it in the sea; then we all begin to laugh.

Pa comes striding along the deck at this moment, smelling of Coal Tar soap and after-shave lotion. He looks rather bristly when he sees me laughing but cannot perceive any joke himself.

"I couldn't imagine where you'd hidden yourself, Ben" he grumbles, "when I came to your cabin to fetch you so that we could watch our arrival at Datça together."

My friends drift away and Pa begins to point out things like the hotel, the harbour and the mosque with its little white minaret, as though he owned the place. I can see all these things for myself, but I prefer just to look at them and dream a little; not to peer at them by order, then listen to their history as well. As you can see, I am still brooding about last evening and in no mood to make friends with Pa just yet.

Luckily Ma comes out on deck to join us and exclaims; "Just look at that lovely beach over there, Jack! You and I will have our first swim from there this morning while your father goes to visit some old ruins."

"Some - Old - Ruins!" Pa repeats in a harsh voice. "Did you not realize, woman, that Cnidus was the headquarters of the Dorian Hexapolis, the town famous for its statue of Aphrodite by Praxiteles, the greatest of all Greek sculptors?"

"No, I didn't, dear," Ma replies with a big grin. "But I'm not nearly as clever as you are, and I shall look forward to hearing all about it when you return."

Partly mollified by this last sentence, Pa leads us down to breakfast where we soon find out that Dorothy and her husband are booked to go on the excursion to Cnidus, but the tall man with twinkling blue eyes (I think of him as the racing-car man) and his wife are planning to explore Datça and go for a swim.

After breakfast a boat comes out from the harbour to fetch us, and some of the women squeak with fear as it plunges up and down beside the gangway. A man with a big curly moustache signals to us to jump in quickly and Ma clings to my arm as we spring for the heaving deck. Another man pushes off with his boat-hook and the little boat goes dancing across the gold-crested waves towards the shore.

"Welcome to Datça - To feel at Home in our Restaurant" says a signboard in English on the front of a house with a wide veranda overlooking the harbour. Behind it the purple and green mountains stretch east and west, and high above us till they touch the edge of the blue heavens; and the white hotel on a small headland, the mosque with its thin white pencil beside it and the gleaming white village all seem to be smiling a special smile of welcome to greet us.

"Doesn't it look a nice place, Ben?" says the racing-car man. "I think we'll have a good time swimming from that beach over there."

"Ach so! But you are very foolish not to visit the marvellous sites from antiquity," snarls the Professor, who is also going ashore in our boat. "Bathing is for children and simple people," his eyes swivel slowly in my direction, like a searchlight hunting for its prey; "but the excursion we shall make today must NOT be missed. Are you aware, my good people," his fat arms make an encircling gesture to include us all, "that the scientist, Eudoxos, the founder of geometry, came from Cnidus? He was the original scholar to apply mathematics to the study of astronomy, and he returned to his birthplace in later years and built there the first astronomical observatory of the ancient Greek world."

Luckily the boat is just coming alongside the stone quay so we prepare to go ashore. Pa joins the coach party who cluster together like a swarm of bees beneath some tamarisk trees. We can still see the Professor's pink noddle rising up in their midst, his jaws working excitedly while his fingers stab the air like frenzied piglets.

"I pity the people of Cnidus!" laughs our friend. "But perhaps it's only inhabited by goats who'll continue to munch their dandelions happily inspite of his presence."

Straight away I know that I shall like Datça. Now that we have landed I can see all the boats in the harbour with their glistening new coats of varnish and white paint; and the little shops filled with many-coloured carpets, brass and copper trays, woolly jerseys, shirts and blouses, leather sandals and brilliant blue, orange and white beads. I can smell meat roasting over charcoal fires, and a sweet new scent that Ma says might be orange blossom, as well as all the country smells that drifted out to sea this morning - the wild herbs and pine trees from high up on the mountain slopes.

Ma buys me a blue and white shirt made of cheesecloth, and a blouse embroidered with flowers for herself; then we choose some marvellous postcards painted by a man called Mehmet Sönmez, to send to all our friends at home.

We wander along the shore till we have left the village behind us, and come to a bay where we can see the racing-car man swimming strongly out to sea while his wife sits on a stony ridge watching him and wondering whether to join him.

"Are you going in, Ben?" she asks me, making room on her bath-towel for Ma and me to sit down.

"You bet he is!" replies Ma. "He can swim like a porpoise and never misses a chance."

I hide among some rocks to change, but a sudden munching noise behind me makes me start; I swing round to find a camel nibbling the leaves on a small tree. I have never seen one outside the zoo before so I stare at him with my mouth wide open; but this makes him rather cross, so he stops eating and turns round to stare back at me.

"Hurry up, Ben. What on earth are you doing behind that rock?" shouts Ma. "Come quickly, or you'll miss a real treat!"

I pull on my bathing-trunks and hurry back to the others just in time to see a beautiful boat, like a great white sea-bird with its wings outstretched, come sailing into the bay. She throws up a sizzling wave of diamonds as she surges through the water. She furls her sails, one by one, then drops anchor in a sheltered corner of the bay, and we all swim out to have a look at her.

"*Hoş geldiniz* (Welcome)!" says the Captain, a big man with

several gold teeth and wiry black fur on his arms and chest. "Please to come on board."

We scramble up a rope ladder and are invited to sit on blue and red cushions in the cockpit, while one of the crew offers us glasses of peach juice; another one fetches us white bathrobes to wear, and the Captain passes round dishes of pistachio nuts and morsels of baby octopus.

"This bay *çok çok güzel* (very very lovely), is not?" he asks us. "Turkey, I hope, to your liking is?"

Ma says that she has never been to such an idyllic place before, and our two friends nod their agreement. "Thank God, we didn't go to Cnidus!" laughs the racing-car man. "Just picture all those sheep trotting along behind the Professor, hanging on his every word."

"That is one very dangerous man," says the Captain unexpectedly, his eyebrows bunched into a straight dark line, like the approach of a thundery squall. Then he tells us how he watched us come ashore this morning while he was preparing his boat in Datça harbour, and how he knew this man to be a brilliant scientist because his reputation had even reached this remote corner of Turkey; but, for himself, he heartily dislikes these types of exalted European professors - always trying to influence poor simple people and use them for Allah knows what evil purposes!

Silence descends on the cockpit after his long speech, delivered with such passion in his funny back-to-front English. But nothing can spoil the beauty of my day and our friends soon change the subject and make me laugh again. Ma, however, seems to have a small cloud hanging over her - an invisible one, because the sky is as clear and blue as ever.

A short while afterwards we thank the Captain for his hospitality and plunge into the warm sea again, to swim back to the beach. The water is so clear that I can see waving leaves from the sea-bed reaching up to tickle my legs, and tiny fish darting to and fro with no fear of this pink monster moving through their world.

I stretch out on the warm pebbles to dry myself in the sun, and close my eyes... Never before in my whole life have I been so happy. Already, after only three days, I have made several new friends with whom I would like to spend weeks and weeks; and this place, this smiling village with the purple mountains behind it, is like heaven. I turn on one side and half-open my eyes: I can see a little white house with a red-tiled roof set on a hilltop; it has a pretty tree in front of it; Ma said it was called a eucalyptus tree - and some big earthenware pots filled with bright pink flowers. A donkey and a goat with its kid are tethered round the side, and I can see a girl wearing a red blouse and baggy blue trousers stretching up to hang the washing on a line tied between the tree and the house.

I close my eyes again and run some pebbles through my fingers. The sun beats warmly down on my body and all my worries about how to cope with ordinary life run out through my finger-tips. For a short while I am just ME - a complete and happy human being with no need to strive to be someone quite different; the sort of person Pa would like to have as a son.

*   *   *   *

The ship is due to sail at two o'clock this afternoon, but we decide to stop at the restaurant which says "Welcome to Datça....", as we still have half-an-hour to spare. We climb up to the veranda overlooking the harbour where I notice the two Turkish gentlemen with their veiled ladies drinking tiny cups of coffee in the far corner. They greet us with friendly waves and smiles and, as if that was not enough, the whole place is suddenly filled with music! Mahmud is standing by the balustrade, his arms outstretched and the words of "My Old Kentucky Home" pouring from his throat. He seems to be floating on a cloud this morning for I have never heard him sing like this before. The racing-car man, who also has a very fine voice, joins him in the chorus, and all the other people in the restaurant pause with morsels of food half way to their mouths, unwilling to break the magic spell by doing something ordinary like eating. And into this unforgettable scene walks the Professor, closely followed by Pa, Dorothy and all the others from the coach party.

It is amazing how quickly a beautiful dream leaves you once you have woken up, and that is how it happens now. Pa has sweat patches on his shirt under the armpits and a red angry face as he strides towards Ma and shouts, "I thought you were taking the child to a beach, not to sit around in a drinking-den listening to people caterwauling!"

Ma turns crimson with embarrassment and looks on the verge of tears, but the Professor, putting a firm hand on Pa's shoulder and steering him towards the entrance, says; "Do not excite yourself, my friend; simple pleasures are for simple minds!" Meanwhile Dorothy titters on the staircase.

"I'd hardly call this a drinking-den," protests the racing-car man, "when no one is drinking anything stronger than coffee or peach juice!"

But the magic spell has been broken and no amount of lighthearted remarks can bring back our perfect morning. We stand in a prickly group on the jetty waiting for the little boat to take us back to the *Zonguldak*. I listen to Dorothy giggling with another woman as they discuss the nude bathers they saw on the beach at Cnidus; and Pa droning on about the amazing lay-out of the streets of the ancient city in the form of a gridiron over a number of terraces.

The afternoon and evening are no better. The ship makes a brief call at Marmaris where the smart yachtsmen and their women trying on clothes in the fashionable boutiques near the waterfront help to dispel Ma's end-of-the-world expression - but only for a short while.

The night is dark and windless, and the hills surrounding the bay of Marmaris are covered with dark trees. I sit on a cargo-hatch looking for lights: there is a small house standing all by itself near the shore with an orange glow coming from one window; the ruby and emerald lights of a ship rushing towards us; and a cluster of distant lights high up on a hill - perhaps from the Greek island of Rhodes?

I have the strangest feeling that I am two separate people this evening. Number One, who has seen bright glimpses of a new world opening up for him since he left home: first, the dancing bear and his master, then his friends on the ship, the present of the lucky blue stone and, most recently, the taste of happiness he had this morning. And Number Two, the same as he was before: quite lacking in confidence, always afraid of people laughing at him and often worrying about some dreadful 'thing' that might happen to him - something he cannot put a finger on but he knows that it would drive him into a twilight world from which there is no escape.

I do so wish that I could be Number One person, for ever and ever.

Chapter VII
Chance Encounters
(Boris's Story)

"You have shown me nothing but trash so far," declares the Master. "Necklaces with which a milk-cow would hardly wish to adorn herself. Let your boy fetch that one I can see on the upper shelf, the one with pure blue beads the colour of the Anatolian sky."

A puff of smoke escapes from his *narghile* as he sits cross-legged on a carpet opposite the shopkeeper, while I wait outside in the courtyard.

"Aha! I see you have excellent taste, *Effendi*, for that is a necklace fit for a prince. May Allah give strength to your purse!"

The shopkeeper orders his boy to bring two cups of tea while the Master examines the necklace and takes another puff at his *narghile*.

"It may be fit for a prince with indifferent eyesight," he muses, "but it has flaws in three of the beads. These I could be persuaded to overlook if the price were reduced sufficiently, for I am a poor man with a hungry bear to support, you understand?"

"A man with such a magnificent bear should be a millionaire," retorts the shopkeeper. "I find it hard to estimate the probable size of the *Effendi's* fortune."

"My bear has sore paws and cannot dance," lies the Master; "but this does not lessen his appetite."

The two men sip their mountain tea and contemplate each other with respect. Presently the shopkeeper sends for a large bottle filled with lemon eau-de-Cologne and squirts it over the Master's head and hands to refresh him.

"I am a man with a soft heart," he asserts; "or I would never dream of reducing such a fine necklace by 10%. But I have no less than nine grandchildren, so it stands to reason that these little ones will suffer with each *kuruss* I forgo."

"Clearly you are a man of noble character," replies the Master, "but it saddens me that I cannot consider your price as I have two aged parents who depend entirely on my support." He rises to leave but the shopkeeper calls for more tea and invites him to remain seated while they discuss the matter in a sensible way.

I feel thirsty and restless so I clatter about in the courtyard until the Master tells me to repose myself, and the shopkeeper orders his boy to bring me a bowl of water and a banana. Thus revived, I doze in a corner until the transaction has been brought to a successful conclusion - no easy task in a town like Kayseri where the merchants are renowned for striking hard bargains.

The Master has a parcel in his left hand and a gleam in his eye when he says goodbye to the shopkeeper and leads me out of the old bazaar, beneath the black walls of the ancient citadel. We stroll along broad boulevards lined with modern apartment blocks, past two monuments of Kemal Atatürk in the busy main square, then on and on till we finally leave the city behind us. The great mountain, Erciyes Dağ, blocks our route to the south-west, so we have to make a long detour before we can reach the land of the 'fairy chimneys', our next destination.

We scramble along the rough track that leads through the foothills, pausing from time to time to gaze at the glowing white peak towering above us. There are fleecy-sheep types of clouds swirling around the summit, and the Master wears a dreamy smile for he knows that we have at last reached the far end of the Taurus Mountains.

This evening we build our camp fire in a sheltered ravine - a place where there are ferns and dried leaves among the rocks to soften our sleeping quarters. The sky is full of stars and the cold Alpine air brings whiffs of myrtleberries and forest animals to tease my nostrils. As soon as the fire is burning brightly the Master unpacks the little parcel, gazes with rapture at the fine necklace he has bought for me, then threads it through my harness in such a way that I shall never lose it.

"There, Boris" he says, standing back to admire me. "Thou resemblest a royal bear tonight, and I hope my little present will bring thee much good fortune in the years to come."

He grills some savoury meatballs over the fire, and we sit on a cushion of pine needles eating our supper under the stars.

* * * *

"The shopkeeper told me that this mountain and its two brother mountains, Hasan Dağ and Melendiz Dağ, were active volcanoes some thirty million years ago, and the soft material called volcanic tufa they coughed up from their bellies was the stuff that formed itself into this amazing landscape."

The Master and I are standing on a hillock gazing across the countryside west of Incesu. The earth is jade-green and ochre-yellow, erupting into the most fantastic shapes: gigantic mushrooms domed with lumps of rock, bananas, cones, rabbit's heads the far-famed 'fairy chimneys' that form this dream landscape which attracts thousands of visitors every year. People are living inside many of these fantasies from which they have carved out rooms, windows and doors, and planted little gardens round the bases; and some have cats curled up on their doorsteps and goats tethered round the back. There are small vineyards and orange, lemon and olive groves in the valleys between the villages, and the great snow mountains away to the south and east.

"Let us find an empty cone for ourselves, little brother," suggests the Master; "then we can stay here for a while and earn some

money to pay for the last lap of our journey."

There are plenty of empty cones in a valley north of Ürgüp, and we select a two-storey residence and settle in very comfortably. We have a tin of wild flowers on our window-sill and some new household utensils that the Master has purchased to make the place seem homely: for instance, a red plastic drinking-bowl for me, a big sharp knife with which to cut up my meat, a stick of bananas from Alanya, a little camping-stove on which to heat our victuals and a short broom for sweeping out our home. One good point I have often noticed about the Master - he seldom wastes money on frivolous things for himself.

We soon develop a daily routine. We get up at sunrise and have a tasty breakfast of fresh cow's milk, bread, honey and bananas, then the Master sweeps the floors in our home and lays fresh straw in my corner, refills my drinking-bowl from a stream that flows through our valley and washes and shaves himself in the cold mountain water as well. Finally, he gives my fur a good brushing and combing, being careful not to touch my new whiskers that are just beginning to grow. I am extremely sensitive on the subject of these whiskers!

We spend the morning in Ürgüp where I dance on a strip of land below the Turban Ürgüp Motel, catching many of the sleepy-eyed tourists who have just emerged with heavy wallets to buy their souvenirs down in the town. Well, they see me first - I am, perhaps, their first impression of Cappadocia as many arrive in overnight coaches from the north - and I save them from wasting too much money among the rapacious shopkeepers down the road.

At midday the Master takes me to a *lokanta* with a shady courtyard, where he orders a sustaining luncheon for us both. I can watch the world go by from this quiet corner, and my favourite sight is a little brown donkey who carries the mobile library round Ürgüp.

He has books piled high on either side of his saddle in two wooden boxes inscribed "Strolling Library Service", and he always brays a friendly greeting to me as he trots past the *lokanta*. Yesterday, when his master stopped for a cup of tea, the donkey and I had quite a long conversation. I found him a most intelligent companion who takes great pride in his profession which, he says, gives pleasure to so many people in this neighbourhood.

I sometimes wonder if the Master might not have had a better life if he had gone to school and learnt to read and write? But perhaps not; his brain might have become too cluttered with this and that, and his generosity and noble character impaired. Who can tell?

After lunch we take a *dolmuş* to Goreme. As you can see we are living in fine style again - like the good old days in Istanbul. The valley of Goreme is the heart of this moon country, this miraculous corner of dreamland. It is really a family of little valleys and ridges, with the scene continually changing as you wander from one to the other. Emerald-green patches of rich crops and miniature vineyards flourish along the valley floors, and the slopes on either side erupt into the most amazing shapes carved from the soft pink and yellow rocks. There are more than a score of ancient churches here, some with beautifully painted frescoes, joined by tunnels, narrow paths and rock staircases.

Many of the inhabitants of Goreme still live inside their 'Fairy chimneys', and some of the ridges of the hills above them wear crowns of reddish-brown earth - Sultan's ridges, I call them.

All these very unusual sights bring the tourists in their hundreds, and we soon gather big audiences who have seen their fill of rock dwellings and crave a little live entertainment for a change Sometimes we make so much money that we leave the main square quite early and stroll around the back, then we give free performances to groups of little children who appear from nowhere with their wide frightened eyes and enormous grins. The life-style in Cappadocia suits us very well, and we might easily have lingered on and lost sight of our original objective to return to our homeland in the Taurus Mountains - but for an unexpected encounter which effects the Master so deeply that he instantly loses his taste for the soft life.

It is late afternoon towards the end of our first week; the magic hour when the shadows stretch their long blue fingers across the sun-warmed earth, and the men come strolling in with their beasts from the fields after a hard day's toil. I have been dancing all afternoon in the centre of the village and I, also, am tired and badly in need of a drink. The Master leads me over to a sandy patch in front of the drinking-trough where a brown and white cow and a small grey ass make room for me. I bow to them in return to show what excellent manners I have.

"You are welcome!" says the cow. "My master has gone to the mosque to say his prayers so I have plenty of time to finish my drink."

The ass says nothing, but kicks a little sand at me with her right hind leg and lowers her long eyelashes. I take this to be a gesture of encouragement, so I move closer to her with a view to nibbling one of her ears.

"Come, Boris, thou hast drunk thy fill! It is my turn now," says the Master, pulling at my collar. Clearly he is anxious to avoid an amorous incident taking place in the main square of Goreme.

We climb up a steep path behind the drinking-trough, and suddenly we come upon an old black Tartar wagon standing outside a house. It has big rear wheels and a blue surround on which is painted a chain of red and yellow roses. It reminds the Master of the wagon in which Zenda used to pull her babies on their long treks up to the summer pastures; and this brings tears to his eyes, so he stands there for a long while staring at the wagon and dreaming. I shuffle my paws and nudge him gently to bring him back to the present, to this friendly village in which we find ourselves this evening. Personally, I would rather go back to the drinking-trough than stand here indefinitely, reviewing my past life.

After a few minutes we descend to a small *lokanta* and squat under a fig tree in a corner of the terrace; from here we can watch the village life without being observed. The Master orders lemon tea for himself and a bowl ofişkembe corbaşi (a soup of chopped tripe and eggs) for me. We are both rather tired this evening, and he looks sad and dreamy as he sips his tea in silence; I try to munch my tripe quietly so as not to intrude upon his thoughts.

The entrance to the museum is opposite our *lokanta*, and a crowd of school children are just emerging with their mistress who behaves like a shepherd trying to round up his flock, then hurries them into a waiting coach. Some of them, however, are rather naughty and self-willed; especially a little girl wearing a red skirt and two younger children, one holding a piece of string with a puppy attached to the other end of it. They run across the road to give their pet a drink at the trough, despite a sharp summons from their teacher.

At that moment the most extraordinary thing happens: so extraordinary that I pause with my mouth full of tripe and stare across the road like a bear transfixed while the Master begins to tremble uncontrollably...

The puppy at the trough has forgotten about his drink because he is far more interested in sniffing at some footprints in the sand; big strong footprints that differ greatly from those left by the hooves of the cows and donkeys who drink there; and the girl in the red skirt, whose shadow is clearly etched against the wall, has her mouth open and tears beginning to run down her face as she kneels on the ground to peer closely at the footprints, her nose almost touching them.

"What on earth has come over thee, child, dirtying thy new skirt in that filthy sand full of the excrement of beasts!" cries the exasperated teacher, running across the road to gather up her missing children.

Slowly the little girl raises her head, sand and dirt clinging to her long dark hair and her face contorted with misery. "Our Boris used to make footprints just like these ones," she sobs to the bewildered woman; "he was our bear, the one I grew up with."

Before she could say another word the Master and I cross the road with one gigantic bound, and he seizes little Djenan in his arms, lifts her right off her feet and swings her round and round and round...

*   *   *   *

We are rumbling along the road to the south in a farm truck, and my Master looks quite different from the one I have known all these years. His eyes are alight with some inner fire and his whole being radiates a strength of purpose, a pressing forward towards a golden target. Our cosy den inside the cone seems far away already, and he has left behind all our nice new household utensils without a flicker of regret.

We pass close to the Rabbit and Bear Rocks and the underground city of Derinkuyu; then I close my eyes to cut out the uncertainty of life and the vast brown plateau rushing past us with the speed of a shooting-star. And I begin to review the extraordinary events of the past few hours.

When the Master had finally released little Djenan who was laughing and crying, both at the

same time, she flung her tiny arms around my neck and began to hug me too! The Master, meanwhile, had come face to face with the very angry school-mistress who demanded to know exactly who he was and how he dared to behave in such a way to one of her pupils - a female child who had been expressly placed in her charge?

After he had explained that Djenan was his own daughter on whom he had not set eyes for five long years, the woman visibly softened and told him how the little girl came to be at the school in Karaman where she herself was the history teacher. Apparently the Master's old mother had been very ill for a long while and no longer able to look after Djenan properly, nor teach her how to cook and weave; so she and her husband decided to send her to school so that she might have the chance to earn a good living when she grew up and, perhaps, to break away from the hard life of the wandering Yörüks. The old man, Abdul Kiazim, searched for many months for a good boarding-school close to the Taurus Mountains so that they could retrieve Djenan during the school holidays; and at last he found the school in Karaman where he brought her three years ago. But last summer he did not come to fetch her, and no message was received via the mountain goatherds who sometimes passed through the town. This caused great distress to the little girl, and had it not been for the kindness of her best friend's parents she would have had nowhere to spend the long holidays.

"I will take her with me at once," declared the Master. "Never again shall she be without a home."

"That is QUITE impossible!" replied the teacher, the severe set of her jaw proclaiming that she was not a person to be trifled with. "We have come on a school outing to see the historic sights of Cappadocia, and I am not in the habit of returning to school minus some of my pupils. You must travel to Karaman yourself to see the Headmaster, if you wish to remove her from our school."

No amount of soft talk nor arguing would make the woman change her mind, so the coach drove away with Djenan's face still wet with tears as she waved to us from the rear window. And immediately she was out of sight the Master began to behave like some shameless foreign tourist, thumbing every passing vehicle until this Allah-sent truck paused to offer us a lift as far as Eregli.

*   *   *   *

"Wake up, little brother, wake up!" The Master's voice intrudes on my dreams. "Guess what that tall mountain is, directly ahead of us?"

I grunt noncommittally, as I was in the middle of a dream and did not wish to return to reality just yet.

"That is the Ala Dağ," he announces grandly, ignoring my lack of interest. "The mountain where thou wast born!"

Well that really does shake the sleep out of my eyes and causes me to stand on my hind legs, peering over the roof of the truck.

"Hold tight, Mr Bear!" laughs the driver, indicating the rough road ahead with a flutter of his fingers. But I hardly notice him, so absorbed have I become in the snow-capped giant on the southern horizon.

The sun will soon be setting behind the Taurus range and our mountain is already tinged with deep blue and purple shadows, the peak glowing like a Sultan's jewel as it rises from the rocky foothills. The Master and I stand side by side in the bouncing truck devouring the Ala Dağ with our eyes and, perhaps, each of us recalling the same episode: the cruel hunters discovering the entrance to our cave where my mother died defending me; Albay, the brave *Karabaş* dog, who first found me; and Zenda giving me some warm milk and honey before she tucked me up with her own babies in the Tartar wagon...

Already the sun has set and the new moon rises above the endless Anatolian plateau; then Venus appears in all her glory, and we draw to a halt outside a café on the outskirts of a town.

"This is Niğde," announces the driver; "and you can just see the outline of the ancient citadel up there, and the three domes of the

Alâeddin Mosque. I always think the minaret looks more like a lighthouse than a tower from which the *muezzin* will summon us to prayer. Let us refresh ourselves with some yoghurt before we tackle the Caykavak Geçidi and the main road to Ankara."

The Master insists on treating our driver to a glass of yoghurt and a plate of *pastirma* (sun-dried beef coated with garlic and savoury spices), and, at the same time, he orders a large slice of *baklava* for me. It is quite dark by the time we finish our meal and climb back into the truck, but the sky is full of stars and the Master points out the Great Bear as we trundle along the road to the south. After a few kilometres the road begins to rise sharply, and the air grows colder and colder.

"Come and join me inside the cab," shouts the driver; "you'll freeze to death out there!"

"You are very kind, *Effendi*, but I would rather stay here with my bear in case he falls out of the truck," replies the Master.

We crouch together for warmth behind the cab and some while later the driver calls out again; "Here we are, on top of the pass, the Caykavak Geçidi. It's 1584 metres high up here."

He slows down, and we stand up behind him to gaze in awe at the dramatic scenery around us. There are wild rugged mountains on all sides of us now, their snow-capped summits way up among the stars. I can hear a distant waterfall singing a haunting song, and the sounds of night animals - perhaps wolves and jackals - born on the wind from the east. I shiver with fear and excitement; it is so strange to come home to these savage mountains after being a city bear for all those years!

Beyond the Caykavak Geçidi we meet the main road from Ankara to Tarsus, the great highway used by all the lorries crossing Turkey and wishing to drive through the Cilician Gates to the Mediterranean coast, then on to Syria, Iran and who knows where. Our truck turns right along this road and the next fifteen kilometres, until we branch off on to the Konya road, are, without doubt, the most terrifying part of the whole journey.

Our truck - I call it ours, for already it seems like an old friend - is a splendid sturdy vehicle, ideal for the farmlands of Anatolia, with an engine that brings a glitter of pride into the eyes of its owner. But it is like a puerile toy compared with the gigantic trans-European/Asiatic lorries, and its lights are but pathetic glow-worms competing against the dazzling searchlights of these monsters. Every few seconds one of them passes us, its driver a ruthless robot, and our poor little truck shudders and swerves while the driver clings desperately to the steering-wheel, his lips forming a prayer to Allah to protect us.

The monsters heading towards Tarsus are, perhaps, the worst for their headlights blind us as they roar slap-bang towards us, heedless of this insignificant midget on their hell-begotten road. I lower my head and lick my blue beads each time we meet one of these fiends, and a feeling of comfort flows through my veins.

The horror of those last fifteen kilometres reduces my Master and me to the consistency of pulped myrtleberries, and we are taken by surprise when the truck suddenly draws to a halt and the driver leans out of his window and shouts "That road leads to Ereğli down the turning to the left. I regret that I cannot take you any further but I am going on to Konya, and this is where our roads divide."

We descend clumsily from the tail of the truck and the Master thanks the man for bringing us so far and insists that he should accept his last packet of tobacco. With a toot of the horn our truck disappears into the night, and the Master and I stand beside the road shivering under the starry sky. I wish I was back in our cosy home near Ürgüp!

It is the hour before dawn, the coldest hour of the night, when we find ourselves on the long straight road to Karaman which is eighty-four kilometres from here. Ereğli in the middle of the night was not a heart-warming spectacle: a few dim lights, nothing to eat nor drink and the only person we saw was a blind beggar sitting on the steps of the mosque where the Master went to offer thanks for our preservation.

I am extremely tired and hungry, but the Master shows no desire to hitch-hike after our experiences on the Ankara road.

"We must keep moving till the sun rises, my poor bear," he says. "If we fall asleep now we shall freeze to death."

We tramp on and on, past marshy land on our right and low hills on our left. The mountains have retreated a long way since we crossed the pass last night, as the road swung north again towards the Anatolian plateau; but each time the Master looks towards the south his eyes light up like burning coals rekindled, and his stumbling feet forget their weariness and advance with fresh vigour.

Three hours later we stagger into the village of Boğeçik and buy a fresh-baked loaf of bread, still warm from the oven, and a litre of goat's milk. What riches after such a night! We find a comfortable ditch on the far side of the village and settle down to devour our breakfast with much smacking of the lips; then to sleep, and dreams of the great adventures that lie ahead of us.

*   *   *   *

"Wake up, little brother! The sun has already crossed the zenith and we must put a good few kilometres behind us before nightfall."

I growl with irritation, stretch my stiff limbs and have a good scratch to delay the moment of departure. I would like to ask the Master if he does not hanker after the lovely breakfasts we used to have in our cone; but that, of course, is impossible, so I grind my teeth and shuffle about from one leg to the other to show that I am hungry again.

"Thou art a truly self-centred bear, Boris, declares the Master. "Think of poor little Djenan waiting for us in Karaman - perhaps with her face pressed against a barred window, hour after hour!"

Suitably chastened, I climb out of the ditch and follow my Master. Already he is striding forward with giant's legs along the hard straight road that goes on for ever and ever. Even if we wanted to hitch-hike today it would not be feasible for nothing passes us, not even a farm-cart nor a string of camels. The sun hides its face behind a layer of whitish-grey clouds and there is nothing to see but the faraway mountains ahead of us, the brown earth encrusted with scrubby green mounds and the everlasting grey road with a white line down its centre.

The air is hot and sultry today and the road hurts my paws; but the Master notices nothing as he plods on and on, with no mention of how we shall procure our evening meal.

An hour later he stops to peer at two black dots on the western horizon, holding a hand above his eyes to shield them from the glare. I catch up with him at last and notice how tired and strained he looks after all those hours on the road.

"I cannot decide whether my eyes deceive me or not," he murmurs, "but I thought those dots were moving a moment ago; then the whole horizon seemed to move, so one can be sure of nothing!"

I squat beside him, indicating that it is time we had a rest; so he also sinks to the ground, his eyes still fixed on the dots.

"They ARE moving!" he announces excitedly; "so I am not crazy after all. They and the long yellowish-brown thing behind them are all on the move, and coming this way."

Well, we sit there rubbing our sore feet and waiting, and a little while later we can pick out two men riding on brown donkeys with a flock of sheep moving slowly across the landscape behind them. Clearly they are devoured with curiosity about the Master and myself! Otherwise why should they lead their flock over here where the pasture is even sparser than where they have come from?

I look far away, at the grey-brown hills beyond them; then back at the flock which has at last arrived. The sheep ignore us, munching noisily at the green tufts by the roadside but the men dismount from their donkeys and walk towards us. The senior shepherd carries a long crook, and he wears an old black coat with a green turban wound loosely round his cap.

"Iyi akşamlar (Good evening)! Welcome to Ayranci," he greets us. "We are very pleased to meet you."

"That honour is mine!" replies the Master.

"We have come to invite you to our camp to share our humble meal."

The Master bows politely and says, "I am very grateful to you for your invitation."

I, meanwhile, shake my fur and cause my ears to stand straight up in points so that my smart appearance will catch the eye of the shepherd and influence him to include me in his invitation.

We trudge across the brown earth behind the donkeys - a pair of pretentious animals, sadly lacking in social graces - and the flock moves with us, their yellow rumps pushing this way and that like the waves on the Bosphorus when it first meets the Sea of Marmara. From the summit of a small hill we can see blue smoke rising straight up into the air beside a cluster of goat-hair tents. My nose begins to twitch and I quicken my pace to keep up with the donkeys.

"That is a very intelligent bear you have, *Effendi*," laughs the other shepherd, a sturdy young man wearing a blue woollen cap pulled right down to his eyebrows. "He knows the meaning of that smoke rising over yonder!"

We are all on excellent terms by the time we reach the camp, and the feast that is laid before the menfolk by their women and female children is a delightful surprise. They have prepared two enormous dishes, one of *kuzu incik patlicanli* (lamb stew with eggplant) and the other of *iç pilav* (rice with pine nuts, currants and onions). And after the shepherds and my Master have eaten their fill, a large bowl is prepared for me. This causes the donkeys to snort with rage; but they must learn that I am a guest-bear, therefore in every way superior to themselves!

The biggest surprise comes at the end: a dish that I shall remember with pleasure for the rest of my life. It is called *kabak tatlisi* (slices of pumpkin soaked in syrup) - a real bear treat.

The Master is sitting happily among the shepherds who have refilled his *narghile* with their own tobacco. It is dark now and the cooking fires are low; thin spirals of smoke arise from the group of men and the sheep snuffle and cough from time to time, while the women chatter discreetly as they wash the dishes. An atmosphere of peace and contentment has settled over the land, a fitting moment to hear the news that will alter the shape of our future lives.

"A party of Yörüks passed this way a month ago," Orhan, the senior shepherd is saying; "and they brought news from the mountains that may interest you, Arif Bey."

The Master has already told them something of his life during the past five years, and of our quest to rescue his little daughter from the school in Karaman.

"They spoke of an old man, Abdul Kiazim, who was once a famous hunter," he continues. "But it seems that he has fallen upon hard times since his son went away to the big city. Perhaps you have come across him during your travels and might know how to get in touch with him? That is why I speak of these matters."

The camp is quite silent; not a blade of grass stirs on the sleeping plateau; then the Master replies in a low voice, "Please, Orhan Bey, tell me everything you know. It is of the gravest concern to me."

So the shepherd tells him of his mother's illness; how she can no longer walk nor weave the fine rugs for which she was renowned in the old days; and how Abdul Kiazim himself is crippled with arthritis in his hips, so he can no longer go on hunting expeditions nor take their goats to fresh pastures high up in the mountains. He has been obliged, therefore, to sell their three camels and many of their fine Angora goats in order to buy bread for his wife and himself to survive. They are living in a cave in the Taurus Mountains on the lower slopes of the Akdağ, somewhere up behind Alanya, unable to travel and desperately in need of the son who left home so long ago.

"Allah in his goodness has surely arranged this meeting, my friends," sighs the Master; "for I would never have known where to look for my family, nor how urgent is my return."

"What a pity you have only a female child," muses Orhan. "You could do with a strong lad to help with the goats and keep the wolves at bay in those mountains."

"My bear will help me to guard our flock," retorts the Master with dignity. "I offer you a thousand thanks for your generous hospitality this evening, but now we must sleep as we still have a long journey ahead of us. "Iyi geceler (Goodnight), and may Allah protect you and your flocks."

*   *   *   *

Chapter VIII
The Eighth Wonder
(Ben's Story)

Mustafa told us this morning that an important general has decided to travel on this ship to Alanya, so she has been ordered to turn west and is steaming back to Bodrum to await his arrival. The Captain looks like a thunder-cloud when he stomps into the dining saloon for his breakfast, and Pa, who also resembles one, is planning to lead a group of grumpy passengers to the purser's office to demand an explanation. They are buzzing like angry mosquitos about missing their flights home, being late for their summer schedules and not having enough time to visit the most important sites like Phaselis and Termessus.

Ma remains seated at the breakfast table with a big grin on her face. "I bet you won't worry about having a few extra days in Turkey, will you, Ben?" she asks me. "I really can't see that it's a matter of life or death to many of these people if they miss this or that heap of old ruins, and get back home a few days late."

"You're not supposed to say things like that, Mrs Merrick!" laughs the racing-car man who is not one of the group heading for the purser's office. "Most people like to think they're indispensable at their jobs."

After breakfast I go out on deck to join my friend, Mahmud the singer, who is standing up in the bows peering at something that puts a secret smile on his face. I lean over the ship's rail beside him and he shows me a beautiful rainbow in the spray tossed up by the ship's stem slicing through the water. Suddenly he grips my arm and points out to sea where a line of dolphins are romping towards us. They look so pleased with themselves as they leap in the air, their bodies wet and shiny and their little round eyes winking at us as they change direction. How I would love to be a dolphin to feel so free and happy! But perhaps they also have mother and father dolphins who tell them what to look at and a whole list of things they must remember to do and not to do?

A crowd of passengers are collecting on the deck behind us, all staring at something on the opposite side of the ship. I would rather keep it as it was before - quiet and peaceful with just Mahmud and me, the rainbow and the dolphins - but these people are all craning their necks towards the coast so I decide to join them.

"That's St Peter's Castle on the promontory, Ben," says Pa, creeping up behind me and making me jump. I had just caught sight of the most romantic-looking castle rising from the rocks in front of a white town.

"It was built by the Knights of St John in the fifteenth century, and I think we shall find it well worth a visit." Pa seems to have recovered from his breakfast-time mood about our change of plans; even to be looking forward to this unexpected port of call.

"Bodrum was built on the site of the ancient Halicarnassus," he drones away happily; "and that was where one of the Seven Wonders of the World once stood. They must have taught you about the famous Mausoleum of Halicarnassus when you were at school, didn't they, Ben?"

I pretend they did, just to please him; although I cannot remember very much about anything I learnt at school nowadays.

"Isn't that THE most glorious castle you've ever set eyes on, dear?" exclaims Ma, who has just joined us. "The judge was telling me that the four towers you can see from here are called the German, Italian, French and English Towers because the knights from each of those countries were responsible for defending their own particular sections of the castle walls."

Pa's eyes become round and bulgy, and he opens and shuts his mouth without letting out a sound because he is so astonished at Ma having remembered these historical facts about the castle. He soon recovers his voice, however, and says; "I think I'll miss the official tour today, and we three can go ashore and explore the castle on our own."

Ma and I feel rather proud and pleased that Pa thinks we are intelligent enough to take exploring with him for a change; and as soon as he is out of earshot she warns me to behave extra well, and to listen carefully to everything he has to say. "At least it's a splendid building and you can tell what it's meant to be," she says; "unlike many of those heaps of rubble he raves about!"

"Vort did you say about robble, Frau Merrick?" asks a silky voice behind us.

Ma becomes stiff and bristly, like a hedgehog in danger - she hates being called 'Frau' and the Professor sends cold shivers down her spine. She grabs my arm and hurries me along the deck, and we soon submerge ourselves in the crowd of passengers waiting for the boats to take them ashore.

*   *   *   *

Today is a day that I shall always remember because it is our happiest 'family' day, perhaps the best one we have ever spent together.

St Peter's Castle turns out to be even more exciting inside than it looked from the sea. We climb up a steep path and go through the outer gate into something Pa calls the North Fosse.

"It's a kind of big ditch, Ben, that used to be part of the castle moat in olden days," Ma whispers.

We wander through a courtyard after looking at some of the ancient cannons, then cross a foot-bridge into the citadel, the heart of the castle. The first big surprise is a brilliant clump of flowers and some lovely trees growing inside the castle walls. The gatekeeper sees us admiring them and strolls across to tell us that

there is almost every type of Mediterranean plant growing here, including some with mythological legends attached to them. He shows us a myrtle, which Pa says was the holy tree of the Goddess Aphrodite; and something very unusual called a mandrake - used for anasthetics at one time. I look up and see a flock of white doves fluttering about in the trees above us; and a peacock ("the greatgreat-grandson of our first peacock here," the man proudly explains) which has such marvellous blue and green feathers that I begin to feel quite sorry for his little brown wife; such a plain bird that no one stops to admire her.

I have just found a monkey on a lead near the souvenir shop, when Pa tells us to follow him into the Chapel of the Knights where the Museum of Marine Archeology is situated. He says it is full of the most interesting bits of sculpture and amphorae, recovered by divers from wrecked ships they found on the sea-bed around Bodrum.

Ma and I have behaved very nicely up till now, listening to his lectures with serious expressions on our faces and looking at everything he wants to show us. Ma, however, suddenly spots a tiny statue of a nude man with a gigantic tool pointing straight at us! She lets out a shriek of laughter and runs forward to examine it at close range.

"Just look at this, dear!" she exclaims; but Pa is not at all amused and hustles us out of the museum before he has had a chance to find the amphorae (whatever they might be!).

There are a number of interesting things to see outside; a Tartar wagon, for instance, in which the nomads used to carry their belongings when they were travelling from one place to another; a huge anchor and a black goat-hair tent, like they still use in some remote parts of the country, the gatekeeper tells us. I crawl inside and squat on a red and blue rug, trying to imagine that I am a nomad myself and this is my only home. It is really quite comfortable in here; there is a camping-stove, bedding and a broom, as well as big cushions to lean against and a low coffee table which makes it seem very homely, although I would never have guessed it from the outside.

"Hurry up, Ben! What on earth are you doing inside that filthy old tent?"

I crawl out and try to tell Pa that it is not at all dirty inside, but there is no chance as he is already leading us up to a grassy terrace where there are statues, some without heads or limbs, growing out of a garden of wild flowers. Bees the size of golf-balls buzz around the flowers, and I can see green lizards darting in and out of the cracks between the stones. Pa points out a white lion sitting on a big stone stand; his two front paws are missing but his legs are resting on iron supports, and he looks so grand and proud that I could stand here gazing at him for ever.

"Hello, Ben! Come and join us up here," calls a voice from the ramparts close to one of the towers. We look up and see the racing-car man and his wife beckoning to us, so we climb up the steep stone steps till we reach the ramparts where there is a wonderful view over the bay. Our friends point out the windmills high up on the crest of a hill, and the boat-building yards where they still build boats to the same designs they have used for centuries. Pa, who is gazing out to sea, notices our ship at anchor on the far side of the castle and a small boat crammed with people just setting off for the shore.

"That must be the Professor's party coming ashore," he observes; and Ma says how nice it is to have the whole castle almost to ourselves - just the five of us.

We climb to the top of the four towers; and Ma gets very excited inside the English Tower as she discovers a relief of a marble lion on one of the walls with some famous coat of arms above it; then she finds the signatures of some of the knights engraved on the window-frames. I want to add my name to them, but both Ma and Pa say "NO", very firmly.

A little further on we come to a round tower that we had not noticed before, tucked away behind the bastion on the north side of the castle. It is called the Snake Tower, and it has a Turkish flag flying from a black flagstaff on the roof. This, I decide, is my favourite tower; it is small enough to be my own personal tower - one that I could defend all by myself if I was one of the knights.

The French Tower has a field of golden-yellow flowers growing at its foot and some strangely-shaped pots, each with twin handles and a round belly, lying about among the flowers.

"Those are some of the famous amphorae!" exclaims Pa; "let's go down and have a look at them."

Well, we squat among the flowers breathing in their strong sweet scent and touching these old old pots with gentle fingers. Some are the colour of pale pink bricks with silvery-green patches of lichen growing on them, and it gives me such a strange feeling wondering about the kind of people who used them all those hundreds of years ago. The sun beats down on the back of my head and I feel sure that I am a Number One person again today.

A few minutes later a herd of chattering tourists led by a fat man with a bald pink head and puffy face come marching into our garden, and it is like a grey cloud passing across the face of the sun.

"Ach so! This is where we find you," exclaims the Professor.

"Just as if he owned us!" Ma whispers in my ear.

Pa looks rather embarrassed and goes into a lengthy explanation about why he decided not to join the group today. The racing-car man and his wife drift away, and Dorothy gives me a spiteful look and moves closer to the Professor. Some dark foreboding tells me that it is important to hear what she wishes to say to him, so I crawl in their direction, pretending that I am still looking at the amphorae.

"You must NOT let that man escape!" she hisses. "We can easily bend him to our will if we detach him from his family, d'you understand?"

"Meine liebe Dorothy, you are fantastic!" he replies, pinching her arm. "Never have I known a woman to do so much for the cause of pure science."

He leers at her in a very ugly way. I do not understand what they are talking about but, despite the hot sunshine, I begin to shiver as I crawl away through the friendly yellow flowers.

"Let's go and visit the famous Mausoleum now," says Ma in a decisive voice. "We can't leave this place without seeing one of the Seven Wonders of the World."

Pa mumbles something about waiting to listen to what the Professor has to say as he is a great authority on the history of the castle; but, for once, Ma has made up her mind and lost all trace of her usual meek nature. She strides towards the entrance, even ignoring the souvenir shop, and Pa and I follow along behind her.

*   *   *   *

Ma read a paragraph aloud from our guide-book, but we are all rather disappointed when we reach the site of the tomb as only the foundations are left, and a few fragments of broken columns lying around among the wild flowers. Inside a small museum there are models of how people imagined the Mausoleum once looked, but Pa says that many of the best reliefs are in the British Museum in London; and when the Knights of St John arrived in Halicarnassus they used the ruins of the tomb as a quarry to supply the stone they required to build their castle.

Because the afternoon has been rather a let down, Ma suggests that we should go to a café on the edge of the harbour and watch the fishing-boats come in while we have our tea. Pa agrees to this plan and they soon find a nice place with coloured umbrellas sheltering the tables from the sun. There are palm trees along the waterfront, a yacht with a big black dog sitting on the cabin-top and another one, like the boat we visited in the bay near Datça, just putting out to sea.

I like this place, and I like the cake dripping with treacle that Ma ordered to go with my peach juice. A few minutes later we are joined by the racing-car man and his wife and the judge without his, and it feels like having a party because everyone is enjoying themselves so much.

After one of Pa's little lectures about the Mausoleum, the racing-car man says; "If you were all allowed to choose an Eighth Wonder of the World, something you've seen yourselves and feel is very special and wonderful, what would you choose?"

He looks at the judge first, who scratches his head while he thinks and thinks: then he replies, "I would choose the sun rising over the Himalayas, seen from a camp in the foothills." His eyes look squeezed-up and far-away as he recalls his wonderful experience.

It is Ma's turn next and she does not hesitate for a moment.

"I would choose an evening dress called "Midnight Rhapsody" created by Christian Dior three years ago," she announces cheerfully.

"Shame on you, Mrs Merrick!" laughs the judge. "I thought this was a serious discussion."

Pa says he would choose the Temple of Bassae in Greece, and the racing-car man's wife says "The edge of the pack-ice up in 80° North." She tells us about the seals and white Arctic foxes, the millions of birds and the emerald and sapphire lights inside the icebergs; and the great silence broken only by the little ice-floes rubbing along the ship's side. And her eyes look just as squeezed-up as the judge's did.

Her husband says he would like two Wonders, as he can't decide which one to choose: either the Gardens of the Generalife in Granada in springtime, or a red Lagonda crossing the Col d'Izoard in the French Alps in a snowstorm. Pa says he can't have two choices, and he replies that he'll have as many as he likes because it was he who invented the game in the first place! Everyone begins to laugh, then the judge remembers that I have not yet had a turn; so they ask me what I would choose.

"For a man with a dancing bear to walk past this table!" I say. Then there is a bit of a silence till Ma calls for the waiter and orders three more cakes.

A few minutes later, when I am busy scraping up the last blob of treacle in my bowl, the judge suddenly holds up a hand and says, "My God, Merrick, that son of yours must have second sight! Really quite remarkable."

I look round, and there is a man striding towards our table with the biggest and finest bear you could possibly imagine pounding along behind him As he approaches us he begins to beat a strange rhythm on a tambourine and the bear rises on to his hind legs; he is so tall that one of his ears gets caught up inside the umbrella. Then the man comes right up to the table and shakes his tambourine at us, at the same time muttering something that sounds like "Give me thousand lira."Pa snarls "Get lost!" and Ma opens her handbag to see if she can find some small change.The judge tells us that it is always fatal to get caught by these sorts of tricksters; and I look at the man's face and realize that something is wrong. He has a red nose and angry red eyes as he shakes the tambourine again, and the bear, although he is so beautiful, seems quite without a heart.

It is terribly embarrassing, but my eyes are full of burning hot tears and they begin to roll down my cheeks. Ma squeezes one of my hands under the table, and at that moment Dorothy and her husband come strolling along the promenade and sit down at the next table to ours. He talks to the bear man in Turkish, perceiving the problem with which we seem to have landed ourselves; and he fixes a price which the racing-car man promptly pays. Then the man with the red nose leads his bear away.

"What's he snivelling about?" Dorothy whispers to Ma, glancing at me with eyes filled with hatred.

"I think it's the wrong bear," she replies reluctantly. Then she looks at her watch and exclaims, "It's after six already! Time we returned to the ship."

Chapter IX

Kidnapped

(Boris's Story)

I am tethered to a palm tree in the middle of the main boulevard in Karaman. A long line of palm trees stretches away to infinity on this island dividing the road in two; and, from my position here, I can observe a number of interesting scenes in the heart of this bustling city.

I can see, for instance, a girl driving a donkey laden with firewood through an archway towards the old citadel; and a fat man, who resembles a tightly-stuffed pillow, is staring at her in an arrogant manner. A great wind is blowing through the streets of Karaman, and the market opposite my tree is filled with babbling women chasing white balloons! No, not balloons it seems, but plastic shopping-bags that have filled themselves with wind and are flying through the air like children's play-things. The stall-keepers shout, the women pursue their bags and the children roar with laughter. I wish I were free to enter into the spirit of this place!

My Master has gone to interview the headmaster of the school. Although he did not mention his reasons for leaving me behind, I suspect that he thought he would present a more respectable figure if he entered this man's den on his own. Well, perhaps he is right, especially after the expensive haircut and shave he underwent in the barber's shop this morning. All the same, now that I have finished my bananas and *baklava* I am beginning to feel rather bored and left-out-in-the-cold, if you see what I mean?

A *jandarma* crosses the road to have a look at me and I grind my teeth ever so gently - just to warn him to keep his distance. His attention is

99

soon diverted, however, by two cars that have had a head-on collision on the right side of the boulevard where the traffic is all meant to travel in one direction; but the man who caused this rumpus drove across the central island to avoid the potholes on his own side of the road! Both drivers are now laughing and exchanging cigarettes, so the *jandarma* swivels his eyes back to me.

I am pondering my next move if he comes any closer when a little pair of arms clasps my neck from behind, and a voice full of love whispers in my ear; "Here I am at last, my own beautiful bear! Now we shall be together for ever and ever."

* * * *

It is hard to describe the explosion of happiness generated by this girl-child with her soft brown hair and eyes that speak a thousand words, without a sound escaping from her throat.

The Master has a miniature tent slung over his shoulders - a parting present to Djenan from her friends at school - and already we are striding along the road to the south with nothing but the empty brown plateau between us and the mountains.

"Thou hast no idea how difficult it was to extract thee from that prison," her father tells her. "The headmaster refused at first to listen to my entreaty, telling me that your grandfather wished you to be educated and had sold three camels to provide for you; and who was I, an unknown *Yörük* dropped out of the sky, to whisk you away in this extraordinary manner? Having had no education myself, I was at a loss for words to defeat his arguments: until an idea took seed in my anxious brain and began to flourish like a sun-warmed melon!"

"What is your opinion of the great leader, *Effendi?*" I asked him, mentioning the name of that noble man who arranged our flight to Kayseri.

"Oh, he is a mighty hero - a man of great courage who has done wonders for his country," replied the headmaster. "But what has this to do with little Djenan?"

Then I told him about our meeting and how pleased the great man had been with my bear's dancing; and how he hoped to meet us again after I had been reunited with my family, as he was planning a visit to the southern Taurus region later this month. Well, that caused the headmaster to change his tune, and to cough and scratch his head while he sought for a compromise.

"Because the summer holidays are so near you can take the child now," he finally conceded; "if you promise to bring her back at the beginning of the autumn term!"

"So that was how we left it, little one," the Master concludes; "and now the whole summer is ours to dance in the sunshine and consider thy future!"

We walk on in silence for a short distance - our pace is becoming slower and slower as Djenan's small legs are not accustomed to striding across Turkey.

"Is that true about us going to meet the great leader?" she suddenly asks her father, fixing him with such a steady gaze that he has no chance to tell a lie.

"Well, it is and it isn't," he replies with a guilty smile. "He did mention his journey to the south when we were at his mother's house. And he told me to call at a certain *lokanta* near the castle in Anamur where he might, perhaps, leave a message for me. So we shall just have to wait and see, my children."

The Master is scratching one of my ears so that I shall not feel neglected; and he soon suggests that we should stop to cook our supper and put up Djenan's new tent, as we are all very tired after such an exciting day.

*   *   *   *

The air, this evening, is filled with magic. Our *kofte* are cooking over a camel-dung fire with Djenan squatting between us, chattering about her school friends and telling the Master how to cook the *kofte* properly! The wind has dropped and the plateau is quite still; the mountains have wrapped themselves in a veil of mystery, and we seem to be the only inhabitants on this earth when we lie down to sleep beside the dying embers of our fire.

I awake at dawn with a cool breeze from the mountains ruffling my fur; I open my eyes slowly and stretch my limbs. It is a clear morning without clouds and the pure white peaks seem only a few kilometres away, their fantastic contours outlined against the rosegold sky. When I contemplate the majesty of this Taurus range and its irresistible beauty, I begin to fear that it may be no more than a dream from which I shall emerge to find nothing but the endless brown plateau sweltering beneath a dun-coloured sky.

"What are you thinking about, my Boris?" asks a soft voice beside me; then two tiny hands grip my right front paw and Djenan turns to watch the red ball of the sun rise above the mountain summits, her face glowing like a rose bush. The Master has collected some camel dung to rekindle our fire, and after a warm breakfast we pack up the camp and set off towards the south.

The mountains may have seemed very close at dawn but it is, in fact, thirty kilometres from Karaman to the Sertavul Geçidi Pass, and a very stiff climb up a zigzag road for the last part of the way. The Master strides ahead with giant's feet that hardly seem to touch the ground, despite the fact that he is carrying all our luggage on his back. But Djenan and I are footsore and hungry after a few hours of tramping across the rough plateau. We stop for lunch and a short siesta around noon, but there are no trees in this

place and the sun is far too hot to allow us to sleep.

The shades of evening have already begun to crowd into the valleys among the foothills by the time we have started on the steep ascent to the pass. Even the Master's pace is slackening, and Djenan has tears rolling down her cheeks as she desperately tries to keep up with us. I can hear the hum of an engine far below us, and a few minutes later we are illuminated by the headlights of a Land Rover. It slows down as it approaches us, and draws to a halt just before the next bend.

"You want a lift to Mut?" asks a foreign-sounding voice from the passenger's window.

"Good evening, *Effendi*. Your kindness overwhelms me," replies the Master. "It would indeed be a great blessing to me and my family to cross the pass in your honourable motor-car."

A man gets down from the driver's seat to open the rear door, and signals to us to get in. The Master whispers to Djenan "I think they must be Jews, judging by the shape of their noses."

He lifts Djenan in first, then climbs up after her and turns round to help me; I am, however, half-way there when I feel my backside being rudely kicked by a steel-tipped boot. I growl with fury but am too late to take my revenge as the doors have already slammed to, and we hear a grating noise like a key turning in a lock. A moment later the driver gets back into his seat, rams the gear lever into its slot and we are thrown together in a heap as the car leaps forward and swerves round the next bend on the rough mountain road.

It is quite dark inside this vehicle and I am exceedingly frightened; and so is Djenan, for I can feel her trembling as she leans against me. The Master is very brave and talks to us in a calm voice about the delicious meal he will order for us when we reach Mut; but he knows as well as I do that we have fallen into the hands of evil men and we shall be lucky to escape with our lives.

The little I saw of the driver was not encouraging. He had closely-crimped oily black hair, the eyes of a cobra and a mouth like a sword-slash in a dead white face. And I shall not forget his ugly steel-tipped boots. I rub my backside where there is a stinging weal from that brute's assault. The two men are jabbering together in their own language now - no doubt planning what to do with us: a bullet, perhaps, for the Master; money to be made from me, either as a pelt for some rich man's hearth or to sell to a zoo; and the white-slave trade for our poor little Djenan. I notice that there are steel bars across the small rear window, and bigger ones combined with a wooden partition dividing us from the driver and his companion. Clearly everything has been carefully thought out inside this devil's car.

Our swaying black prison becomes colder and colder as the Land Rover climbs to the top of the pass. I can see patches of snow through the rear window and, finally, a notice-board which says Sertavul Geçidi, Rakim 1610. The engine stops its breathless snarling and we are thrown violently against the front bars; then the car goes hurtling downhill with the screeching of tyres at each bend in the road, and the sound of stones being dislodged and sent flying over the edge of a precipice.

"It's a pity it's night-time and we're travelling so fast," says the Master, to divert our attention; "for this is one of the most beautiful routes through the Taurus Mountains. Far below us is the Göksu Gorge with a winding river flowing through a narrow defile. Up here, near the pass, the country is very wild and wolves and bears roam freely, but further on the valley widens out and it would be filled with orange and lemon trees heavy with fruit at this time of the year."

His voice trails away and Djenan continues to tremble, although she tries hard to disguise this weakness from her father by squeezing closer to me. Perhaps she fears that he will regret having rescued her from school if she behaves like a scared baby, but she and I understand each other perfectly; neither of us is made of very brave material and we find it impossible to live up to the Master's standards. I can see his profile outlined against the night sky at this moment, and he looks as tranquil and indestructible as a granite boulder.

The Land Rover slows down and suddenly we see the lights of a roadside café in the rear window; then more lights - rather dim ones from the houses of a large village clinging to the mountainside.

Simultaneously, the Master points out the silhouette of a fortress on the right side of the road.

"This is Mut already," he whispers; "perhaps we shall have a chance to escape here."

But the car does not stop in the village. It has, in fact, already begun to speed up again, brutally throwing us from one side of our prison to the other as the driver jams his foot hard down on the accelerator and chucks the Land Rover around the hairpin bends.

"We must escape very soon, my children." The Master's voice sounds tense and serious at last. "If we are still inside this box when we reach Silifke, the driver will turn left and head for the Syrian border and we shall have no hope. So we must escape up here in the mountains when the car swings round a bend, for that is the only time it goes slow enough not to kill us. These bars are too strong to move - I have already tested them; so you and I, my brave bear, must prise up the floor-boards to make our escape through a hole in the chassis! And there is not a moment to lose."

He begins to loosen a board with his knife, and as soon as he has prised it away from its brother boards I wrench it out with my front paws. Praise be to Allah for the wooden partition between us and the villains, and the noise this hell-cart makes as it thunders along the road. After the fourth floor-board, a gap appears beneath

us and stones shoot through this aperture to hit our faces like shrapnel. I put down my right fore-paw to steady myself on a fat metal tube just below me... and let out a roar for the thing is filled with fire!

"Boris, that's the exhaust pipe!" I hear the Master's voice dimly through a haze of pain. "Come quickly, my children, before the driver stops to find out why thou didst roar."

The brakes squeal as the Land Rover approaches another bend, and the Master pushes Djenan through the gap, telling her to jump clear of the rear wheels. He grabs me round the shoulders next, and hauls and pushes me with all his might - I am too busy licking my injured paw to take any active part in our escape. And, finally, just as the car leaps forward to speed down the next stretch of straight road, the Master himself emerges, his arms flailing wildly to grasp the branches of a bush growing on the edge of a precipice.

At last the night is still - still and silent, except for the sounds made by the Master and Djenan crawling towards me. Their faces and hands are covered in blood and bruises, but the Master's eyes are bright and urgent: "Thanks to thy great strength, my brave bear, we have escaped," he whispers; "but we must move away from the road with the utmost speed in case the villains return."

He puts my left fore-paw round his shoulder to haul me out of the bush in which I landed, and Djenan throws an arm round my waist on the other side; thus supported, I stagger up the steep rocky slope, step by painful step. It is very hard for me to climb using only my hind-paws, what with the darkness, the thorny undergrowth and my throbbing fore-paw. I have begun to feel extremely sorry for myself when a gruff voice above me says "Good evening, Mr Bear!"

I look up in astonishment and perceive an aged tortoise sitting on a stony ledge, observing me with shrewd eyes.

"I watched your adventures from my terrace," he continues, "and it is important that you listen to my advice. There is a cave at the side of this giant rock where you must hide immediately, in case those human devils return. I will come for you when the coast is clear and lead you to a track across the mountains where you will be safe from all demons on wheels."

The Master and Djenan of course cannot understand our conversation; but they sense its importance and follow behind the tortoise till we reach a small cave, its entrance almost invisible behind the branches of a juniper tree. We sink exhausted on to the dank earth at the back of our refuge, and Djenan tears a strip of material from her white head shawl, spits on it to make it cool and binds it very gently round my injured paw.

The tortoise, meanwhile, is hovering near the entrance with his eyes trained on the road, when we hear the hateful sound of that snarling engine coupled with squealing brakes.

"Keep total silence!" he commands, shuffling away through the undergrowth to observe the ruffians' next move.

The sound of guttural voices speaking in low-pitched angry tones drifts up to us in the cave; the engine snorts again and, suddenly, the whole place is flooded with light as the car swings round sideways to illuminate the mountainside with its headlights. We hardly dare breathe, but I lick my blue bead necklace and pray that my huge footprints will not lead them to our hiding-place.

The wise tortoise had clearly foreseen this possibility and devised a brilliant scheme: he has moved some distance away to one side of the cave and, directly above the bend in the road, he dislodges a heavy stone which clatters noisily down the bank. The Jews leap in the air with surprise, then creep on stealthy toes towards the source of the disturbance, the leader holding a sawn-off shotgun in front of him. The tortoise lurks under a myrtleberry bush to keep an eye on their movements, while the Master, Djenan and I remain frozen to the back of the cave; our heartbeats are so loud that I feel sure they will reveal our whereabouts.

The men, however, are too busy trampling about in the bushes to stop and listen; also the night is black and stormy and the sound of a pack of wolves howling among the upper crags has a daunting effect on them. The driver relieves himself, growls some bitter words at his companion and spits disgustedly into the bushes; then the two thugs worm their way down through the dense undergrowth, jump into their Land Rover and slam the doors shut. Two minutes later they have gone.

"Stay calmly where you are for five more minutes in case it is just a ruse and they decide to return," counsels the tortoise, his comfortable shape appearing at the entrance to the cave.

I convey this order to the Master by stretching out my bandaged paw to block his exit. The minutes pass very slowly indeed and I can still feel our little girl trembling with fear, so I wrap my other fore-paw around her shoulders to comfort her. But all is well, and a few minutes later I hear the tortoise singing a special song in a squeaky voice outside the cave:

"Have no fear
The coast is clear,
The villains have fled
And now to bed!"

Chapter X

The Oracle

(Ben's Story)

I am a Number Two person again today. No one has said so, but I can feel it in my bones and in the way that people avoid looking at me - even Ma and Pa.

The purser stands up in the dining-saloon during breakfast to announce that the General will come aboard at ten o'clock tonight, and we shall sail at midnight; so we are to stay in Bodrum for one more day. Before anyone else has a chance to suggest a different plan, Ma gives Pa a certain look and says, "Let's try and hire a taxi to explore the Bodrum Peninsula and take Ben for a swim. I believe there are some lovely beaches near here."

Pa looks a bit put out but says he does not mind having a swim, although he had rather hoped to join a group going to Priene; but if we went ashore straight away, he might still have enough time to fit in both excursions.

My beautiful Turkish lady and her husband are standing on deck talking to Mahmud, and they wave and smile at me as I go down the gangway. Dorothy's husband strolls across to the taxi-rank to help Pa arrange the price with a driver; Dorothy, meanwhile, sits under a palm tree staring at me as if I were a piece of driftwood washed up by the waves. I am glad when Pa has fixed everything and we can climb into the taxi and drive up the steep hill out of Bodrum.

The peninsula turns out to be a glorious place full of wild flowers and windmills. We drive inland through a white village where I can see a man leading four camels over a small bridge. Tall yellow flowers sprout on either side of them, and there is a white mosque in the centre of the village and a cluster of white houses with red-tiled roofs.

A few miles further on we have to do a big swerve to avoid a pair of rams fighting each other in the middle of the road; then we slow down and draw to a halt beside a river, and the driver asks us to get out as he has something "*çök güzel*" to show us.

"I think that means 'very lovely'" Ma, who has learnt a few words of Turkish, tells us. "Let's see what it is that he's pointing at in the water."

A harsh noise grates on our ears and Pa observes "Frogs having an argument!"

Then we all peer into the water and see some mud-coloured creatures the size of table-tennis bats floating around serenely. They seem rather shy and, when one of them catches sight of us, he floats away under a water-plant so that we can no longer see him. The driver says "*Çök, çök güzel*" and Ma says "It's the first time I've seen a turtle out in the wilds. They are rather special, aren't they, dear?"

We drive on across the peninsula to the north coast, through a village called *Türkbükü* where boats are being built in the middle of clumps of flowers; and I can see some men standing on a jetty slapping strips of wet leather against the side.

"That's not leather, Ben," Pa corrects me; "those are octopuses, and that's how the men kill them as they have very tough leathery skins."

I do not like the idea of this at all, but I soon forget about them when we reach the beach where we are to bathe. The sea is shimmering with marvellous emerald and sapphire lights, and a few small boats are fishing off the rocks on the far side of the bay; but there is absolutely no one on our beach - it is like a private beach belonging to some famous pop star!

Well, Ma and Pa and I go swimming and I am having a lovely time; and the sea is so warm and friendly that I could stay here for ever. But all too soon Pa's voice comes booming across the water, "Time to go now, Ben; better come back and get dressed."

Ma, who has covered herself with sun-tan oil and is happily sun-bathing on the beach, opens her mouth to protest; but nothing comes out because she has just remembered how unselfish it was of

Pa to bring us on this expedition, and she knows how much he wants to visit Priene.

We bundle into the taxi with our wet bathing-costumes and skins tingling with sun and salt water, and the driver sets off up the steep winding road leading to the crest of the hills. The engine coughs and splutters occasionally, and it gets hotter and hotter on the back seat. Pa, also, has started fanning his face with his Panama hat.

I can see the family of windmills now, like a row of big bee-hives crossing our route at the point where it reaches the crest. Smoke is beginning to squirt from under the car's bonnet, and behind us there is a trail of smoke puffs blotting out the view of the countryside. The engine hisses and groans, louder and louder, and suddenly it gives a deep sigh and stops completely - like someone falling asleep in the middle of a sentence. The driver leaps out and throws open the bonnet, then springs backwards into the ditch while the engine behaves like a boiling kettle that has rid itself of its lid. His eyebrows shoot upwards till they meet the shaggy hair on his forehead, and he flings his arms out wide and cries *"Bozelmuş!"*

"Bozelmuş," repeats Pa; "what the hell's the fellow talking about?" Then he turns to the driver and says "Garage?" - very loud and clear.

"Garage yok (there is no garage)," the man replies, wiping the sweat from his face with the sleeve of his jacket.

"Telephone?" tries Pa, his eyeballs bulging with exasperation.

"Telefon yok (there is no telephone)." The driver stares at Pa as if he were a child, and Pa looks like someone about to burst a blood vessel.

*   *   *   *

A powerful engine has been labouring up the hill in front of us for some while, and suddenly a coach appears over the brow and draws to a halt in front of our taxi.

"Mein Gott!" declares a hateful voice through one of the open

windows. "You poor people; we have come just in time to rescue you!"

Ma, who has gone to visit one of the windmills, comes running out to say that we do not need rescuing and we cannot leave our poor taxi-man in the lurch just because his engine has broken down. Pa cuts her short rather nastily and hustles us into the coach while he pays off our driver. Two minutes later we are rumbling back along the road to the north once again, hemmed in by all the people I like least from the ship.

"What a VERY lucky coincidence!" Dorothy purrs at Pa from further along the coach. "We were all so sorry that you were forced to miss the expedition to Priene, and here you are after all!"

Ma looks as if she had just swallowed a sour prune. Other days I should have wanted to laugh, but not today. I feel frightened of some evil spirit inside this coach, and even the sight of a donkey with its baby walking by the side of the road does not help to make me smile.

We drive on over a dull green plain, and I notice that Dorothy has changed her seat and moved up front to sit beside the Professor where they are whispering to each other at this moment. Pa burbles aloud from his guidebook about the history of Priene, and another place called Didyma where something known as an oracle lived inside the Temple of Apollo, and used to give the most amazing answers to all the really important questions it was asked by the ancient Greeks. Ma, meanwhile, stares out of the window looking remote and sulky.

Some while later we cross a muddy brown river which excites most of the people in the coach. "That's the Meander River!" Pa announces in his know-all voice; "and this is the Great Meander

Valley, a famous place in olden days."

The coach puffs slowly uphill after the river, and a mountain appears ahead of us which has a fortress on its summit. It is called Mount Mycale, according to the judge's wife, and it stands guard over the remains of the ancient city of Priene. As soon as the coach stops, everyone leaps out and begins to climb like a herd of mountain goats - everyone except Ma and me. Pa soon disappears from sight, but she and I move slowly up the track to the ruins, stopping to pick a bunch of flowers on the way. At last we reach a flat terrace full of lizards darting in and out of crevices in the rocks and bumble-bees buzzing around the flowers. It is a lovely place, we tell each other, and there are pine trees dotted here and there and five columns standing in a row at the foot of Mount Mycale.

"That's the Temple of Athena," says a breathless man, who had run back to the coach to fetch his camera and is now on his way back up the hill. "Isn't it a perfect gem!"

He is out of earshot before Ma has a chance to reply, but we can now see the people from the coach crawling about among the ruins all over the hillside.

"It's always like this," Ma sighs, wiping her face with a handkerchief. "Let's scramble up a bit higher, dear, and see what your father's up to."

We climb higher and higher, over marble chunks and fallen slices of column, till we arrive at a small gateway leading into an enormous theatre.

"It used to hold six thousand people..." Ma begins to tell me, but suddenly her teeth clamp together and she forgets what she was about to say. I follow the direction of her eyes and see a flowering shrub growing out of the old stone seats on the far side of the theatre; it almost conceals three people who are huddled together and so deep in conversation that they do not notice us. Ma jerks my arm and pulls me rapidly back through the gateway.

*   *   *   *

The journey back to Bodrum is dreadful. Pa hardly opens his mouth till the coach turns off down a side road leading to some more ruins at the place called Didyma: then he mutters something about paying a lightning visit to the Temple of Apollo, and orders Ma and me to remain in the coach. This makes her extremely angry, especially when she sees Dorothy scuttling after him.

This temple does not seem to make him any happier, however, for he comes back after a short while looking as if he'd seen a ghost and refusing to answer any of Ma's questions; so we travel in total silence all the way back to Bodrum. I sit by myself in the bows of the motor-boat that takes us across the harbour to ZONGULDAK, and I gaze at this beautiful town and wonder if I shall ever come here again.

I decide, later, to do some serious eavesdropping to try and find out what happened at Priene this afternoon. Ma and Pa are hardly on speaking terms and I feel far too anxious to wish to sleep. After telling Ma that I am very tired and want to go to bed early I return to my cabin, undress and get into bed. Some while later I hear her creeping along the passage, and she opens the door very gently and stands there listening to see if I am asleep. I have pulled the sheet over my head and am breathing regularly and rather noisily, so she closes the door again and creeps away. Then I hear her and Pa in their cabin next door, beginning to have an argument.

"I have made up my mind now, and there is to be no turning back," he says in a firm voice. "After all, it's for the child's own good, and just imagine how marvellous it will be when we get him home NORMAL!"

"I don't agree with you. He's quite alright as he is and I, for one, don't want his character changed. I don't trust that old German snake further than I can see him: whatever induced you to get mixed up with such a wicked louse?" Ma's voice has risen to a high

114

pitch, and I can hear her beginning to sob.

"Calm yourself, Lucy," Pa speaks harshly. "I have told you before that the man is a famous brain specialist and, as a great favour, he is willing to operate on Ben . So we shall leave Turkey the day after tomorrow, flying from Antalya to Munich where the Professor will take the child straight to his special clinic; then we shall go back home and wait to hear from him."

A silence ensues, broken only by the sound of Ma sobbing and blowing her nose. Then Pa speaks softly to her: "I never told you what happened during our brief stop at Didyma, did I? Well, I got out there specially to ask the Oracle what we should do. I never really expected an answer, mind you, as one doesn't exactly believe these old tales from Greek mythology. But the most extraordinary thing happened: after I'd asked my question, an unearthly type of voice somewhere at the back of the temple whispered these words; "Have the courage of thy convictions and never let a chance to improve thy children's lot escape thee."

For a whole minute there is complete silence; then Ma inquires in a bitter voice, "Did this oracle speak in English, then?"

"Naturally, you stupid woman," Pa snaps; "otherwise how would I have understood her?"

"Funny to find an English-speaking oracle in Turkey, and a female one at that!" Ma slams the door behind her and stomps off along the passage.

*   *   *   *

Well, now I know everything, and have only a short while to think about it before we leave Turkey and I become a different person.

I get dressed, go out on deck and sit on one of the lifebelt lockers near the stern of the ship, gazing at the foaming white waves galloping along behind us. My mind is quite blank until Mustafa finds me and sits down beside me with a hand on my shoulder, to show that he will not allow me to jump overboard. His hand makes me want to cry, because it tells me that he understands and would like to help me - not to change me into a different person, like other people want to do.

Chapter XI

The Letter

(Boris's Story)

The sky is pink and grey above the mountains and I open my eyes for a second, then close them tightly. I am sitting under a big tree with my fore-paws crossed in front of me, and in that first moment of waking I have an extraordinary vision; a small brown female bear with her back to me is disappearing into the dense woods on the far side of the track! I open them again and cough encouragingly but there is nothing to see - absolutely nothing except the Master and Djenan lying fast asleep on the ground beside me.

It was our wonderful friend, the tortoise, who brought us to this dirt road leading across the mountains to Gulnar. We are now, however, quite alone once more and I have been wondering how we shall ever find our way to the coast.

Djenan, who was still wearing her small haversack when we escaped from the Land Rover, opened it just as the tortoise was saying goodbye and pulled out a young lettuce which she presented to him. Seldom have I seen a brother animal weep with pleasure as that old tortoise did!

*   *   *   *

I must have dozed off for a minute or two because, the next time I open my eyes, there is a man with a string of camels standing there staring at us. His gaze is so penetrating that the Master stirs in his sleep, then opens an eyelid for a fraction of a second; but long enough to release the vocal chords of this stranger who is clearly most anxious to ask us some questions.

"Good morning, my friends!" he addresses us; "I see that you have had plenty of trouble during the night with all those bruises and dried blood on your hands and faces; and I grieve for that poor bear of yours with a bandage round his paw?"

The Master, who is never slow to respond to a friendly word, returns this man's greetings and tells him about our adventures the previous night.

The stranger then declares that it would please him if we would care to call him Süleyman, and inquires in which direction we are travelling.

"To the Mediterranean coast, somewhere near Anamur," the Master tells him.

"Ah, that is most fortunate for I myself am going to Aydincik, so we can travel together for part of the journey. I think that your bear and little daughter are in no condition to walk very far, so we shall let them ride on one of my camels whose saddle-bags are empty at present; and you and I can walk beside them?"

We are all charmed with this proposal - all except the camel. I have noticed before that these animals have inferior manners and do not really appreciate a hard-working bear when they meet one. This beast is no exception, but he is compelled, notwithstanding, to kneel so that Djenan and I can mount. It is a big adventure for her, and she sits on the camel's neck while I ride behind with my forepaws clasped round her waist to hold her in position. Suddenly the beast rises to his feet and sets off at a good pace with the Master and Süleyman trotting along behind us.

Our journey lasts for two days - two of the happiest days you could wish for. Süleyman is well known along this route, and whenever we pass through a village there is a friendly welcome awaiting us and plenty of good simple country food. My paw still throbs miserably under the bandage that Djenan soaks in cold water and replaces, time after time; but I can now eat plenty of young azalea roots, myrtleberries and honey, so my fur grows sleek and glossy and I feel an overwhelming surge of amorous desires!

That vision I had on the first morning was no fantasy after all as I have seen that young bear more than once today, and each time she gives me the most inviting looks when she suddenly appears among the thick foliage that hems us in on either side. But what can I do, perched on this grumpy old camel's back with Djenan and the Master to protect?

Another of Süleyman's camels is a female with her baby running beside her, and every so often we have to pause while she suckles the little one. I have to admit that he is a charming youngster, who has not yet had time to develop any of the less attractive traits of these types of animals. Although so young, this infant camel wears a fine blue bead necklace and a red bow which gives some idea of the generous character of our new friend, Süleyman.

I spend the first night in the crowded backyard of the inn at Gülnar where the atmosphere is heavy with the smell of dung and the incessant chatter of camels and donkeys - not a stopover I would recommend to other bears travelling this way!

The countryside changes after Gülnar, and Djenan cries out with delight when she spots our first wild roses growing like stars among the small pine trees on the lower slopes of the Taurus Mountains. The air is filled with the scent of flowers and the song of the bumble-bees; and after a little while Djenan also begins to sing - very softly so that only I can hear the words. Her song tells the story of a boy who is lost and far from home, and his heart is sad and lonely till he meets a beautiful Yörük girl tending her goats; then she takes him to her tent...

"Where didst thou learn that song, my little one?" asks the Master, taking us both by surprise. "It does not sound the type of lesson they would teach thee in that school at Karaman!"

Djenan's face has turned as red as a poppy, but her father is laughing as he drops back to continue his conversation with the camel-driver.

Late on the second afternoon we arrive at

Aydincik, and part from Süleyman and his camels with great sadness.

"Thou hast truly been a heavensent friend to us," the Master tells him; "and may Allah protect thee on thy journeys across the mountains. It would give me great pleasure if thou wouldst accept this knife as a small token of our friendship?"

Djenan and I are on the ground by this time - our camel knelt without too much persuasion to release us - and I cannot refrain from giving a low growl when I see the Master giving his knife away, as I happen to know that it is one of his most prized possessions from the days of his youth; also it is his only implement with which to cut up our meat.

"Boris, can I never teach thee how to behave!" he sighs, as we set off along the coast road in the twilight. "When someone has done so much to help us in our troubles, how could I not give him something in return? And, as thou knowest, all my other possessions remained in the Jews' car. One day, perhaps, thou wilt offer thy blue bead necklace if the occasion should demand it?"

My only response to this is a deeper growl. I am not inspired by such noble feelings and I would HATE to part with my beautiful necklace!

We do not wish to sleep in a town tonight as we all prefer the open countryside; so we plod on along the road to the west till we come to a long sandy beach with fat white pebbles scattered across it.

There are some abandoned fishermen's huts on the edge of the sea which pleases Djenan very much, as she lost her new tent during our escape and is not yet accustomed to spending the night out in the open.

After supper - only bread and bananas this evening - we curl up on a wooden platform inside one of the huts and go to sleep: but it is not until next morning that I begin to sense the magic of this place. The waves are pounding on the beach with a steady rhythm and, mingling with their haunting song, I can hear the voice of the *muezzin* in a neighbouring village calling the faithful to prayer. At times it is hard to tell one from the other, but the Master has also heard the *muezzin* and he creeps out of the hut so as not to wake Djenan and walks away towards the sunrise where the holy man is singing his song.

I lie on my back for a long while listening to the frogs croaking in the river that runs into the sea nearby, and seagulls shouting with glee as they hover over the breaking waves. The air is full of salt spray and Djenan wakes up and runs into the sea with her arms outstretched like the wings of a bird. I watch her from our hut and wonder whether I aught to plunge in after her, but I am no water-beast so feel quite relieved when I see the Master striding along the beach clutching a parcel.

"I have brought my children something special for breakfast!" he announces happily. "Some bread fashioned in the French style to resemble a new moon. The baker says they call it 'croissants' in France."

Djenan comes back from the sea, dripping like a wet sponge with a big grin on her face, and we all squat on the beach to eat our special breakfast. The Master spreads some butter and honey over my what-d'you-call-'ems, and they taste so delicious that I close my eyes and guzzle very slowly, to store up the memory for leaner days.

When we have finished we wash our hands and faces in the river, then set off along the coast road to Anamur.

*   *   *   *

This road is very beautiful - more so than any I have travelled along before. On our right side are the mountains, with great scars and pinnacles of red rock touching the blue heavens - real bear country with plenty of caves and much to eat when a bear feels hungry. And on our left lies the turquoise-blue sea, bright and

smiling this morning with a million diamonds glittering in the water under the warm rays of the sun.

After a while our road turns inland and mounts higher and higher, through pine woods filled with rock-roses, orchids and cow-parsley. Later we pass through some banana plantations (what joy to eat a banana whenever you feel hungry!), then olive groves and sweet-smelling mimosa.

The road curves back to the coast again, and we reach the outskirts of a village where a woman is emptying rubbish into a dustbin. She wears a striped red and blue jersey over black trousers and has a big smile on her face when she sees me, so I do a little dance in front of her. "Good morning, *Effendi*" she greets the Master. "What a charming bear you have! Please come to my house so that I may give him some *lokma* (doughnuts in syrup)."

Djenan takes hold of my fore-paws and dances me round and round, and the woman laughs and claps her hands and urges us to follow her. When we reach her house I perceive a charcoal grill that is already hot and smoking and, perhaps divining the drift of my thoughts, she threads some slices of young lamb and bay leaves on to a skewer and puts them on the grill to cook; then she looks up and notices the Master and Djenan standing there, so she prepares two more skewers as well as a dish of *Imam bayildi* (this means the Imam fainted because it was so delicious!). It turns out to be the most excellent meal that this angel-woman serves us, but when it is time to leave and the Master is expressing his appreciation I know, instinctively, what is passing through his mind. His eyes are fixed on my blue bead necklace, so I hastily think of a way to outmanoeuvre him: I spring forward into the road and do my very best cha-cha, despite my damaged paw and the Master having lost his tambourine. And we make our exit on a note of glory, for the woman has assembled her children and neighbours to watch me dance, and everyone is clapping and laughing as we fade away down the road to the west.

*   *   *   *

It took two long days to reach Anamur; but here we are at last, limping towards the great Crusader castle in a land inhabited by the descendants of pirates - a dark and sullen race who greet us with the utmost suspicion. The Master and Djenan sink, exhausted, on to chairs in the garden of the *lokanta*, while I squat in a corner and try to make myself inconspicuous.

"Please bring me a banana and two glasses of peach-juice," the Master tells the waiter. Needless to say, he has hardly any *kuruş* left in his pocket - certainly not enough to buy us a meal.

The waiter regards us with an insolent gleam in his eye and I have a strong desire to bite him! But I restrain myself for a moment as the Master is asking him a question.

"You have not, by any chance, received a letter or message for Arif Bey from our great leader (he mentions the man's name), have you?"

There is a pause: time stands still for a few seconds while a score of different emotions pass across the waiter's face. Then he bows slightly and says, "I will fetch His Excellency, the Proprietor."

We wait in the garden in anxious silence, suddenly conscious of our shabby appearance after so many days on the road. I watch a bee buzzing round a pot of marigolds; then a fat middle-aged man comes out of the restaurant holding a letter in one hand. A surprised look appears in his dull brown eyes when he perceives us.

"My waiter informs me that you are Arif Bey and this is your dancing bear?" he says, ignoring Djenan completely. "I have been entrusted with this letter and a request that I should give you a meal while you read it."

The Master raises his hands to protest and say that we are not hungry, but the Proprietor announces that our meal has already been paid for and he has some excellent *'Bonfile'* (fillet steak) that he specially recommends. I lick my lips in anticipation and Djenan

does the same while she tickles one of my ears; but the Master merely nods his head, all the while clutching his letter as if it contained a priceless jewel.

As soon as the Proprietor has left us, the Master leans forward and grasps Djenan's hand. "Read it to me, child!" he implores; "thou hast education and can understand these strange symbols."

Djenan opens the letter and picks out the words, one by one, with a frown of concentration on her face. She is not a great reader despite her three years at school, but this is what she finally tells us:

My dear friend, Arif Bey,

I have often pondered on our meeting at Reşadiye, and the manner in which your very intelligent bear entertained me. I was particularly struck by something in your own character, certain qualities that are rare nowadays, as rare as gold-dust if I may say so.

Because of this I have an offer to make you which I hope you will not refuse. An old uncle of mine died last year and left me a small piece of land with a stone hut on the beach in a remote corner of the Gelidonya Peninsula. It is of no use to me as I am always busy with the affairs of my country, and when I grow too old for these matters I shall retire to my village of Reşadiye where I was born. But for a man who is not afraid to work, there is enough pasture for a herd of goats on the surrounding hills and the fishing is excellent on that part of the coast.

Being a Yörük, you may not wish to settle in one place; but go, first, and look at this land, Arif my friend, and spend a few days there before you decide.

Wishing you good health, great happiness and a long life,

Your sincere friend,

P.S. I have had a word from the Governor of the Southern Taurus region that your old parents are well, and filled with happiness now that *they know you will soon be with them again.*

A coaster called Mehmet Aksoy leaves Alanya with cargo for Finike every Wednesday, and will take you close to the bay where the little house is situated. When you receive this letter, please go there first - the ship will bring you back to Alanya a few days later - before you disappear into the mountains to search for your family!"

The waiter has already brought the 'Bonfile', accompanied by a mountain of fried potatoes and a green salad, and Djenan and I are eating ravenously. After the first few mouthfuls, when I have taken the edge off my appetite, I look up and notice that the Master has hardly touched his food. I glance at his face, wondering if he has a fever; but no, there is something else - some new expression that I have never seen before. It reminds me of the sky in early springtime, with fast-moving clouds chasing each other across the face of the sun.

"How would it feel to have a home of our own, my children?" he asks us excitedly. "And some land to cultivate and a flock of fat Angora goats!"

Before Djenan has time to answer, however, the pendulum has swung the other way and he asks in an anxious voice if we should not ignore such day-dreams and set off towards the Akdağ immediately, in search of his mother and father?

Djenan, who has finished her lunch already and feels strong and clear-headed, perceives the problems tugging this way and that in the Master's mind and says; "Eat thy food, my Father, then I will read the letter to thee again. But I think thou wouldst offend this noble-hearted man if we go wandering off across the mountains when he has taken the trouble to find out that Grandpa and Grandma are well and know that thou hast not forgotten them."

He nods his head thoughtfully and begins to eat. Djenan and I, meanwhile, hold our breath and wait to see what will happen next. We both want to go immediately to this dream-place by the sea, but we dare not push the Master too far in case he feels that he is no longer in charge of the situation and the pendulum refuses to swing back.

The waiter reappears at this moment, bearing three large slices of *baklava*, and I forget our problems during the total bliss of the next few minutes. When I have licked the last fragment from my bowl I look up again - and the Master has gone.

Djenan clutches her sides with laughter; "Didst thou not see him leave, thou greedy thoughtless bear? He has gone to say his prayers in the mosque inside the castle, and we are to follow him there and hear his decision."

We leave the garden of the *lokanta* and cross the road to the beach where Djenan hunts for sea-shells and throws sand over me until I chase her back on to the road; then we walk solemnly into the grounds of the castle. What a gigantic place it is with its great ramparts and many watch-towers, the ones on the south side guarding the remains of an ancient harbour. There are large empty spaces within the walls where grass, flowers and shrubs grow at random, and a small mosque arises like an island out of the wilderness.

No signs of the master yet, but a coach has just drawn up at the eastern gate and twenty or thirty American tourists descend and come crowding through the archway. They have several guides - local boys seeking their favours - in attendance, but I am accustomed to dealing with such vultures so I spring forward with a roar to galvanize the foreigners' attention. Djenan - meanwhile, beats her hands together in a steady rhythm to make up for our lack of a tambourine, while I rise on to my hind legs and begin to dance.

I get carried away with all the clapping and cheering from these simple people, while the guides grind their teeth with fury but dare

not interfere. By the time the Master emerges from the mosque with a serene smile lighting up his face, Djenan and I have already earned a nice sum of money. We bow to our audience before leaving the castle, and one old lady runs forward to tie a rainbow-coloured scarf round Djenan's neck and blows a big kiss in my direction!

"I see that thou hast been well employed during my absence," the Master laughs and scratches my ears, "so I have made up my mind to please my children. We will go straight to Alanya and find that little ship to take us to the place by the sea!"

*   *   *   *

It is a hundred and twenty kilometres to Alanya but, with so much money in the Master's pockets, we are able to ride in the bus all the way there. What luxury it is, squatting on a soft seat with the turquoise sea gliding by on one side and fields of poppies and fennel under the olive trees that lead up to the mountains on the other.

The bus stops for ten minutes in the ugly town of Gazipaşa where the Master buys us a bag of mixed nuts; then the rumbling wheels start turning again, along the endless straight road leading towards the sunset.

An hour or so later the driver looks over his shoulder and shouts; "Anyone for Alanya?"

The Master puts up his hand, so we draw to a halt in front of a big hotel and he jumps out and helps Djenan and me to climb down the steep steps.

"Iyi günler!" calls the driver as he pulls away, while we stand in the middle of the road waving to him.

"He's dropped us on the wrong side of the town," the Master tells us; "so we'll have a long walk to get to the harbour. But never mind, my children, it is Tuesday today and thanks to thy big earnings, we have arrived in time to catch our ship which leaves on a Wednesday. Come, let us move before the sun sinks behind that high promontory over yonder which was once the pirate's main stronghold on this coast."

We walk through the city, past grand hotels and fine shops, and cafés and *lokantas* by the score. Djenan wants to stop and peer into all the shop windows, but the Master urges us on and on till we come to a small shipping office on the far side of the town. A clerk is standing outside in the street closing the shutters for the night, but the Master hurries towards him and asks; "Please, *Effendi* tell me what time the *Mehmet Aksoy* leaves tomorrow and allow me to buy three tickets?"

"She leaves at four o'clock in the morning," the man replies, "and it is lucky you did not come a few minutes later or I should have gone home. There is no charge for your bear, and half price for the little one."

He has a kind face, this shipping clerk, and the Master is in the middle of expressing his thanks and paying for the tickets when Djenan calls out; "Do come quickly, Father; there's a big white ship steaming into the harbour!"

We hurry along the jetty towards an enormous passenger liner - just like the ones the Master and I used to see from Galata Bridge in Istanbul. As she draws closer Djenan spells out her name - *Zonguldak*, and we squat on a low wall to watch the sailors fasten her ropes to the shore.

Then a most extraordinary thing happens: I glance up at the front end of the ship which is much higher than the middle, and notice someone waving to me; but not just ordinary waving, for this boy looks quite desperate and very unhappy. Suddenly it all comes back to me, this is the boy we met so long ago in that park in Istanbul, who had such a deep-throated laugh right from the belly and who shared his melon and honey-buns with us!

I nudge the Master in the ribs - he is gazing dreamily out to sea - then stand up and wave back with my left fore-paw, swaying to and fro on my hind legs to give a stronger effect.

"Look, Father!" cries Djenan, who is always quick to detect my meaning. "There's someone waving to us from the ship."

At last the Master looks up and stares at the boy for a long while without speaking. The sun has already dipped behind the great promontory, and the purple shadows of evening are fast closing in.

Chapter XII
The Last Port Of Call

(Ben's Story)

During the coldest hour of the night, just before the dawn begins to break, I go back to my cabin and try to sleep. I toss and turn, count sheep running through a gate, lie on my back then on my tummy; but it is hopeless because I feel as if a swarm of bees was buzzing round inside my head. Time is getting so short now - only one more day on this ship where I thought I had found the way to the stars, then we shall leave and never return here again.

I think of all my friends: Mustafa, Mahmud, the beautiful lady who gave me the blue stone to bring me luck (I put a hand up to my neck to make sure it is still there), the racing-car man and his wife, and the bear with his master in that park in Istanbul. Suddenly I begin to cry again, so I bury my head in the pillow in case Ma is listening.

I get up very early and go out on deck to watch the waves galloping past us. They are blue grey, sizzling white and gold - gleaming waves that remind me of other waves and other mornings when I was almost a Number One person.

I can see some purple mountains away to the north, but ahead of the ship there is nothing but the endless blue sea. After a while I go right up into the bows - to the place where Mahmud was standing when he showed me the dolphins only two days ago. This morning there is no Mahmud nor dolphins, and no rainbow in our bow wave; but when I turn round, there is a stranger standing with his back to me gazing out to sea. He is big and square with grey-white hair, and he is wearing a smart navy-blue suit. I think he must be the General who came aboard in Bodrum last night.

Breakfast sticks in my throat. We are due to arrive in Alanya late this afternoon so Pa gives the other people at our table a lecture about the old fortress there, but refuses to meet my eyes; and Ma, who has a wet Sunday expression on her face and puffy red eyelids, seems too upset to look at anyone.

There is one curious thing I notice, however, when we are out on deck between breakfast and lunchtime: Ma, who has washed and powdered her face by then, appears to be making a special effort to get to know a new lady who came aboard last night; Mustafa says she is the General's wife and speaks perfect English because she went to school there when she was a girl.

All my friends sense that I am very unhappy today, and they do their best to make me smile. Mahmud sings a special song for me, and the lady who gave me the lucky stone keeps on drifting by and squeezing my hand; last time she ran her fingers through my hair and said a few words, very softly. The racing-car man chatters away to me during lunch, and mentions all the things he knows I like; but Pa drones on and on about the history of Alanya, and Dorothy stares at me with half-closed eyes glinting like ice-cubes, so my throat feels dry and I cannot think of anything to say myself.

"The rock on which this pirate's stronghold was built is almost three hundred metres high," Pa declares; "and it was called Kalonoros, or 'beautiful mountain', by the ancient Greeks. When we arrive there," he turns to Ma, "I think there'll be enough time to climb to the top and do some exploring before we start our packing."

"I don't want to!" I say very firmly, without really knowing why I opened my mouth.

There is a big hush. No one moves for a few seconds, then Pa replies in a loud bossy type of voice; "Rubbish, Ben. A stiff climb will do you good and give you a better appetite for dinner."

Soon after this we go out on deck again and Pa strolls across to talk to the Professor. As soon as he is out of sight, Ma sits down beside the General's wife and they begin to chatter like a pair of budgies; then I see her open her handbag and scribble something on a piece of paper which she gives to this lady, at the same time glancing over her shoulder to make sure that Pa is not watching her. I wonder, vaguely, what she is up to but am really far too miserable to care. By mid-afternoon most people on deck have moved across to the side where the coast of Turkey lies, and are gazing at a big hump that looks like a whale's back. It is very hot and hazy out here, but as we draw closer I begin to pick out a few details on this hump. It is made of reddish-yellow earth dotted with small trees; and I can see houses - mainly white houses with red roofs; and crenellated walls and watchtowers, almost the same colour as the earth, running along the shore and zigzagging up a steep hill till they reach a castle right at the top. It looks an exciting sort of place, and I would love to go exploring all over that hill some other time, but not today.

There is a blue boat moving in towards the jetty where people are standing around waiting for our ship. I notice these things without much interest - even the pilot-boat that came out to meet us did not excite me like all the other ones have done.

I walk along the crowded deck and up towards the bows to join Mahmud who is perched in his favourite position, getting in the way of the sailors who are trying to moor the ship. He beckons to me urgently - as if he had something special to show me; so I run to him and lean over the deck-rail beside him...

I can see a group of three sitting on a low wall watching *Zonguldak's* arrival: there is a man wearing a grubby cloth cap, a sheepskin waistcoat over a grey woollen shirt and a pair of baggy black trousers, with a little girl beside him and, squatting on the ground between them, a big brown bear!

I stare and stare with my mouth wide open, hardly conscious of Mahmud who is laughing and saying something to me. Suddenly I feel quite certain it is them, inspite of the girl; so I stand on a bollard and begin to wave. The bear spots me first, and I can see him nudging his master; then he stands on his hind paws, swaying from side to side, and waves back to me; and so does the little girl. She wears a bright red skirt and her face looks very pretty from here.

At last the man looks up and catches my eye. He sits there quite motionless, staring at me with such a gentle expression on his face.

*   *   *   *

"Ben, I've been hunting everywhere for you and I couldn't find you." Ma is tugging at my sleeve, her face all tear-stained again.

I jump down from my perch beside Mahmud as I do not want her to see the group on the jetty. We go back to our cabins and I notice that she has started to pack my suitcase. It does not matter any more, so I help her to squeeze everything in. When we have finished she says, "Come and watch the boys diving. Your father has gone with the others to visit the fortress but I stayed behind to be with you."

Suddenly I feel happy and strangely excited. I want to kiss Ma because I love her very much and know she is on my side. But I cannot explain any of these things to her in case she should become suspicious, so I just smile a little and follow her out on deck.

There are three boys diving off the high jetty to find coins that people are throwing to them from the ship. They are marvellous divers and I would like to join them as I am pretty good myself; but I decide it is better to stay where I am. I can keep an eye on the group ashore from up here - they have not yet moved from the low wall - and these boys have given me an idea.

Some while later Pa returns from the fortress with his friends, and I watch the steward standing at the top of the gangway checking everyone in and out. The General and his wife have already left the ship. Ma waved them good bye from the lower deck - and now it is nearly time for our last meal.

"It's to be a gala dinner tonight, Ben," Pa shouts through the cabin door, "so you'd better wear your smartest clothes."

Well, I dress up in my navy-blue trousers and my shirt with the Ferraris whizzing across it, and we go down to the dining-saloon which has been decorated with paper garlands

131

and balloons. Everyone except Ma seems to be in a party mood, offering wine to each other, wearing paper hats and eating plate after plate of the delicious food the chef has prepared for us. The Captain stands up and makes a short speech, first in Turkish then in English; afterwards we all clap, then go through to the lounge where the dance-band is tuning up.

I slip out on deck for a moment to see if they are still there. Yes, thank the Lord; the girl is curled up on the ground fast asleep beside the bear, and the man is still sitting on the wall gazing out to sea.

It is three o'clock in the morning now, and I dare not wait any longer in case the night becomes the new day. I have had an ear pressed to the next-door keyhole for ages; Pa is snoring loudly, but I cannot hear a sound from Ma which worries me.

I have put my shoes inside my haversack which is firmly strapped to my back, and I open the cabin door ever so gently and creep along the corridor on tiptoe. I stop at the corner to look back and listen but there is not a sound. I move faster now, down another long corridor towards the front of the ship, then out on to the cargo deck at last.

No time to pause and think; otherwise I might change my mind and never do it. I climb up on to the ship's rail, touch my lucky stone with one finger, then put my hands together straight out in front of me and... one, two, three, I've gone!

The shock of hitting that black cold sea, the darkness, the weight on my back and the water rushing into my eyes, nose, ears and mouth nearly kills me. But suddenly I rise to the surface and know quite clearly that I want to live; so I strike out towards the jetty which looks as tall as the cliffs of Dover, but I remember that there are some steps somewhere - if only I can find them.

A light flickers briefly above me and I hear a girl's voice calling me; so I swim towards this magic sound and there are the steps at last. They are very oily and slippery, but a pair of strong hands reach out to grasp my arms and drag me out of the sea.

It is nearly five o'clock now - my watch has not stopped inspite of its plunge into the sea - and I am sitting on the cargo hatch of a little coasting ship called *Mehmet Aksoy*, watching the most beautiful sunrise I ever saw in my life. One of the sailors has lent me a shirt and trousers to wear while mine are drying in the engine-room, and another has brought me a big mug of tea. It tastes of flowers and lemon-juice - not at all like our tea at home - but it is wonderful, all the same.

The bear-man sits on one side of me with eyes like friendly purple grapes - just as I remember them when Ma rushed me out of that park - and the little girl has soft brown hair and is very shy, but I know that she does not hate me. The bear keeps on jumping around in front of us to make me smile; then he shows his big yellow teeth and scratches his armpits, and I laugh till my ribs ache.

And far astern of us I can see the pink whale's back of Alanya fading away into the distance.

Our voyage lasts for a day and a night - a grand voyage with plenty to eat and drink, and this warm feeling all around me which I cannot yet explain.

Soon after sunrise the following morning we moor up in a tiny harbour surrounded by blue mountains, and get ready to go ashore. The captain of our ship has a long talk with the bear-man, and his hands fly about, right and left, as if to indicate some special path we must follow. We say goodbye to all the sailors who have been so kind to us, then we step ashore and set off along the coast road towards the morning sun.

It is a marvellous day with far-away mountain summits merging with the pale pink clouds. There are orange and lemon trees on the right side of the road, and I can see the turquoise-blue sea

glittering through their branches. Boris - that is the bear's name - jumps up and shakes a branch so that some oranges fall to the ground; then Djenan the little girl, picks up the four best and gives one to each of us.

Well, we go tramping along this road for several hours, and all the time I can sense a mounting excitement in my companions. I am not sure why this is, but every so often we stop and the bear-man pulls a torn piece of paper out of his pocket and hands it to Djenan and she lays it on a rock and stares at it, then says a few words to her father. We have been climbing for the past half hour and suddenly the road swings sharply round a corner. A big black goat coming the other way collides with us, then it all begins to happen...

First, there is an enormous dog. He has a short cream-coloured coat, black ears, a grey-white muzzle and sad brown eyes. He is limping badly and I think he must be a very old dog; but, at that moment, he springs forward and puts his front paws on the bear-man's shoulders and begins to lick his face.

"Albay! Albay!" the man whispers, and I can see tears running down his cheeks while he hugs the dog as if he were a child.

Boris, meanwhile, looks rather grumpy, and so does the goat who is munching flowers beside the road. Then I look up and see an old old man leaning on a stick, who has come quietly round the corner and taken us all by surprise. The bear-man and Djenan run to him and kiss his hand, and I turn away to watch Boris who is pretending to bite the dog's left ear - they look like old friends to me, and seem to be having a wonderful game.

I am beginning to feel a bit left out of things when the bear-man takes me by the arm and presents me to his father. The old man puts a hand on my head and says a few words which I cannot understand; but it does not matter because I have the most amazing sensation flowing through my veins that I am a Number  One person again, and will soon become part of this family who will never forsake me.

We follow the old man along a stony track that curves round a shoulder of the mountain, and suddenly he raises his right hand and stands quite still. The bear-man, Djenan, Boris, the dog, the goat and I crowd together behind him, and we see a little stone house with a red-tiled roof and one chimney. It has enormous pink and blue mountains up behind it, and small trees at the back all blown by the wind towards the mountains; and there are red and yellow flowers in front, and fat white boulders at the bottom of a grassy slope that leads down to the sea. And the water is the most wonderful blue-green colour you could possibly imagine!

Well, here we all are, staring at this little corner of paradise. The bear-man's face has lit up like the sun peeping over the mountains, and his daughter is dancing the bear round and round, faster and faster. The old dog is sitting close to the old man, and they both seem to be smiling as if they shared some particular secret. Even the goat looks more cheerful, and he has already started trotting down the track towards the house.

Then an old lady comes to the door and waves a soup-ladle, and we all start running down the track...

Epilogue

Lucy Merrick sat under a tree in the park reading her letter. It was a cold winter's day and the wind swirled the fallen leaves around her feet, but she was oblivious of her surroundings. For the first time in many months her plain white face was alight with a radiant glow that brought a smile to the corners of her mouth - like the early flickering of a candle-flame that would grow stronger and stronger as the wax warmed up.

She gazed into space for a few minutes, painting a dream-picture in her mind from the words she had devoured so hurriedly; then she fastened her fur collar more securely round her neck against the icy wind-fingers, and began to read the letter very slowly, word by precious word...

*   *   *   *

Ankara
12th of November

My dear friend, Lucy,

At last I have news for you which I hope will bring you some peace of mind.

But first I wish to thank you for your letter to me, and to say that the few things my husband endeavoured to accomplish to help you were nothing compared with the extraordinary courage you displayed on that fatal night last year. To stand there at the porthole watching your only son jump overboard, and not to wake your husband nor raise the alarm because you knew in your own heart that this was Ben's best chance of survival, seemed to us to be the ultimate sacrifice of a truly noble spirit. So the small gesture my husband made in causing the police inquiries into Ben's disappearance to be conducted with less vigour was the least we could do to help a very brave lady in distress. We did, I must admit, have great difficulty in shaking off that evil professor and his English accomplice - a daughter of Satan that woman must surely be! But your poor husband was too devastated by the loss of his son to cause much trouble.

Let me now share with you my special news and the impressions of our journey last month. My husband had some inspections to make in the south-western corner of Turkey so we reserved two or three days of freedom, just for ourselves, and set off to follow some leads given us by an old friend, the captain of a cargo ship operating on that part of the coast.

We drove from Finike along the main road towards the east, running beside a lonely beach where you can see the outline of the Gelidonya Peninsula far away in the distance. It is a wild and beautiful place where the waves come thundering into the bay, throwing up clouds of iridescent spray as they break on the beach and I had this sudden premonition that it was the most perfect prelude to what was about to follow...

A few kilometres further on we came upon a herd of Angora goats which were just about to leave the main road and take a rough track on to the peninsula. We soon found the goatherd, before a Yörük with a gentle demeanour, and an old Karabaş dog who was busy guarding his master in no uncertain terms! Well, this man was intelligent enough to realize that we had not come to make trouble for him, so he led us over a spur of the mountain to a point where we were suddenly arrested by a marvellous vision...

How I wish that you also could have been there with us, Lucy, in that first moment when we looked down into the little cove. It was an enchanting place, quite sheltered from the sirocco, and our eyes immediately fastened upon an old stone cottage with a red-tiled roof and smoke curling skywards from its one chimney. A few tamarisk trees and a low wall round the back to form an enclosure for the goats completed this miniature property, and there was a sturdy boat drawn up on the foreshore with some fishing-nets laid out to dry beside it. The sea in that cove was just how you would love it most - a shimmering bowl of water filled with turquoise and sapphire lights!

As we approached the little house I noticed a very pretty girl sitting on a stool in a corner of the enclosure working at a carpet-loom, and the rug that she was weaving was a perfect example of the Yörük women's ancient art. Straight-away we ordered one for our own home.

An old old man, who resembled the pictures of your prophet, Isaiah, then appeared and invited us into the cottage with such dignity that I felt most humble in his presence. It appears that he was once a famous hunter called Abdul Kiazim from the Taurus Mountains; and the goatherd is his son - the same man whom you saw so briefly in that park in Istanbul when you first came to Turkey.

It was spotlessly clean inside the house, and we sat cross-legged on fine Yörük rugs spread across the floor while a frail old lady and the girl prepared a meal for us.

"Well, what about Ben? Where is he and why does this woman ramble on in this maddening way?" I can hear you saying, dear Lucy! You must be patient for two or three more minutes, then I will tell you.

The reason that I have described the place to you in such detail is because this is where your Jack now lives; and from what I could gather from the family, he works tremendously hard and seems happy and contented, what with the fishing and the goats to tend and the bear... Yes, I had forgotten about that famous bear, but he plays a very important part in their lives as he still dances whenever an opportunity presents itself, and helps to swell the family income with his earnings. In fact, it is he who has been responsible for them buying the herd of goats; and this in turn has given them plenty of milk and cheese, and the valuable Angora wool for making their rugs and clothing. There had been a festival in a local town that very day, and Djenan had taken Boris across the mountains to dance there.

Well, everything sounded fine so far; but it was all hearsay, and we wanted to SEE Ben for ourselves. We agreed with Abdul Kiazim that it would be better not to reveal to the boy why we had come at this stage, but the family sensed our anxiety and Djenan the little girl, suggested taking us to a hiding-place just above the cove, from which we could watch his return.

My husband and I were soon ensconced in the upper branches of an umbrella pine - we felt like school-children, I may tell you, and we had not been there more than a few minutes when a figure came striding over the spur leading a rather tired bear behind him. He was wearing a broad floppy hat, a smart jacket and leggings with good strong boots, and he carried a rucksack and blanket on his back and a tambourine and long stick in his left hand. He had a springiness about his step and a look of purpose in his eyes that amazed us.

As he swung round the spur, the girl came running towards him and the family were standing outside the cottage waiting for him. For one fleeting moment I caught a glimpse of his face and I wish I could describe to you, dear Lucy, the glow of happiness that shone in his eyes.

So that is all I have to tell you today, my friend; but we wait for the day when you will decide to come back to Turkey and we shall lead you to your Ben and all his friends, not least that wise old bear, Boris!

Your devoted friend,

Fatima

Glossary

"Allahahasmarladik!"	*"Allah go with you!" (Goodbye!")*
Amophorae	*Greek or Roman 2-handled vessels -sometimes found on the sea-bed.*
Baklava	*A pudding of flaky pastry filled with honey.*
Bey	*A Turkish Governor. Polite way to address someone.*
Börek	*A flaky pastry filled with herbs and meat.*
Bozelmuş	*To break down (a car).*
Çiçek	*A flower.*
Çoç çok güzel	*Very very lovely.*
Dolmuş	*A taxi in which all seats may be filled.*
Effendi	*A Turkish title of respect applied to government officials and members of learned professions.*
"Garage Yok"	*"There is no garage."*
"Güle Güle"	*"Smilingly! Smilingly!" (Reply to "Allah go with you!").*
"Hoş geldiniz!"	*"Welcome!"*
Iç pilav	*Rice with pine nuts, currants and onions.*
Imam bayildi	*The Imam fainted (because this dish was so delicious!).*
Işkembe corbasi	*Soup of chopped tripe and eggs.*
"Iyi akşamlar!"	*"Good evening!".*
"Iyi geceler!"	*"Goodnight!".*
"Iyi gunler!"	*A polite expression when you are saying "Goodbye" to someone.*
Jandarma	*Police, 'Gendarme' (in French).*

Kabak tatlisi	*Slices of pumpkin soaked in syrup.*
Kemel Atatürk	*The great dictator who westernized modern Turkey.*
Köfte	*Meatball.*
Kuruş	*A small Turkish coin.*
Kuzuincik patlicani	*Lamb stew with egg plant.*
Lahmacum pide	*Flat bread with minced meat, onions and tomatoes.*
Lokanta	*A restaurant.*
Lokma	*Doughnuts in syrup.*
"Merhaba!"	*"Good-day!" "Hello!"*
Muezzin	*A Mohamedan crier who proclaims the hours of prayer from a minaret.*
Narghile	*Oriental tobacco pipe, with smoke passed through water.*
Pastirma	*Sun dried beef coated with garlic and savory spices.*
Raki	*A very strong Turkish spirit drink.*
Yaşmaks	*White veils worn by Moslem women.*
Yoğurt	*A fermented liquor made from milk.*
"Yok"	*"No; there is not".*
Yörük	*A Nomad member of a tribe who wanders from place to place, looking for pasture for their goats or sheep. A wanderer with no fixed abode..*

Other books by Rozelle Raynes

Each book is fully illustrated with photographs
and the author's own drawings

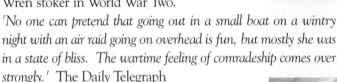

MAID MATELOT

This is the third edition of a book where
Rozelle Raynes relates her adventures as a
Wren stoker in World War Two.

*'No one can pretend that going out in a small boat on a wintry
night with an air raid going on overhead is fun, but mostly she was
in a state of bliss. The wartime feeling of comradeship comes over
strongly.'* The Daily Telegraph
ISBN 0954746708   paperback   £6.99

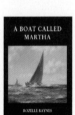

THE TUESDAY BOYS

The story of eight boys from East London who
grew up together in Care, and their adventures
aboard Rozelle Raynes' Folkboat 'Martha
McGilda' as she taught them all about sailing.
*'A book which will delight and entertain...and it will move
the reader deeply.'* Yachting Monthly
ISBN 1871482062   hardback   £10.95

A BOAT CALLED MARTHA

Rozelle Raynes vividly describes over forty
years of sailing 'Martha McGilda'.
*'Will entrance all lovers of sailing and boats. In
fact, the author's sheer delight in what she does
and her wonderful way with words makes this a very enjoyable
book for all readers, even for non sailors.'* The Wren
ISBN 1900289474   hardback   £15.00

27 KISSES

The Last Coach from Croatia

A unique, true story of four homeless families from the former Yugoslavia who escaped to England, and of how the author and her husband made a home for them. A moving and frequently amusing tale narrated in the author's usual highly descriptive and personal style.

ISBN 1871482143 paperback £7.95

LIMEHOUSE LIL

and that small corner of London's docklands where she ruled supreme... until Canary Wharf arose

An evocative look at how Limehouse used to be. Rozelle Raynes' wonderfully descriptive writing, her moving, poetic and frequently hilarious accounts of what the area has meant to so many, brilliantly captures the heart of this part of England's capital.

ISBN 0954746716 paperback £7.95

All available to order from bookshops or direct from Thoresby Gallery, Thoresby Park, Ollerton, Newark NG22 9EP (telephone 01623 822465/822009) or email gallery@thoresby.com. If ordering from Thoresby Gallery cheques should be made payable to Thoresby Gallery. Credit/debit cards accepted. If paying by cheque please add £2.50 for postage and packing regardless of how many books ordered. Thank you. For card payments £2.50 will be added to your transaction for postage and packing.